BLOOD TIDE

By Brent McGregor

DUAL CROWS PRESS

Sydney, Australia
MMXXV

DUAL CROWS PRESS
Spinning tales of terror and make-believe.
Sydney, Australia
MMXXV

ISBN 978-0-6453400-4-4

Cover design by LimeSpringStudio.com

PRAISE FOR BRENT MCGREGOR

"Blood Tide is brutal, bloody and tense...This book is one hell of a ride, and will keep you turning the page until you reach the end, out of breath and exhausted."

Alister Hodge, Horror Writer

"I'm tired today because I had the pleasure of reading an advanced copy of Blood Tide, and it kept me up all night. If you're looking for a murder/ mystery with a supernatural element, check this out." Pauline Yates, Horror Writer

"This darkly compelling read lured me in and wouldn't let go. Ominous and grisly. In 'Blood Tide', McGregor pulls the monster out from under the bed, then flings it at you. And you'd better run. Because it's one vicious, unstoppable nightmare of a thing." Jeff Clulow, Horror Writer

"McGregor thoroughly introduces and defines his people and his worlds without losing pace or the readers focus." (Not this book) Scott R.S. Raphael, Horror Writer

"Extremely well written...A really enjoyable read of the weird and supernatural..." (Not this book)

Cheryl, Goodreads

"So gory and twisted with fantastic imagery. Still shuddering at the ending." (Not this book)

A.M. Joseph, Horror Writer

Books by Brent McGregor

1. Blood Tide
2. Strange Murmurings
3. Denizens of Darkhaven

For Amy and Roxanne.

"Black Jack Davey came a riding through the woods
And he sang so loud and gaily
Made the hills around him ring
And he charmed the heart of a lady, he charmed the
heart of a lady" — The Carter Family

PROLOGUE

Ron Dunlop pulled the lapels of his sailing jacket tight to shield himself from the lashing rain. He swayed as the boat rocked. Above him, high winds moaned like a banshee in the rigging.

He studied the horizon with an intense stare, his craggy face and calloused hands evidence of the many miles he'd put under the keel. Some people considered him old for a mariner. Then again, some people didn't know their ass from a hole in the ground. He was mentally sharp, in decent shape, and he would keep on sailing well into his seventies—if Margaret would let him.

They'd been holidaying in Martinique on board their sailing yacht, the *Halcyon Daze*, headed for Barbados, when, despite the morning's forecast, the horizon became dark and ominous. A storm hit without warning, barring their way. So, they beat a hasty retreat to the island of St. Lucia, taking refuge in a sheltered lagoon somewhere along the rainforest-covered coastline.

They'd dropped anchor and had stowed most of the gear below deck, when…

"Ron!" Margaret called.

"What's up, Hon?" He let go of the tripline. They'd been married for 42 years, and he could tell, from her tone, something was amiss.

She wore a sailing jacket like his and had a timeless, natural beauty. When he looked at her, he still saw the young twenty-something woman he fell in love with, all those years ago.

"There…on the beach." She pointed. "I could've sworn I saw a man."

He looked in the direction she pointed but saw nothing.

"I don't think so, hon," he yelled over the wind. "This part of the coastline is remote. There's not a town for miles."

"I know what I saw," she yelled back. "There was a man. He waded into the water and hasn't resurfaced."

"Are you sure?" he said, looking again.

"He could be drowning, Ron."

"He could be a diver."

She frowned.

"Perhaps you imagined it—a mirage, or a trick of the light? Maybe it was an animal?

"An animal, Ron? What kind of animal?"

He shrugged. "A feral pig or goat."

She gave him a look.

"Heck, I don't know. Your guess is as good as mine. Look, we've got to get below deck."

By the time the storm rolled back around, they'd already bunked down for the night.

***

Ron woke with a start. Margaret had him by the shoulders and was shaking him. The cabin was dimly lit, but he could still make out her frightened expression.

"Are you okay?" he said, sitting up.

She shushed him. "Do you hear that?"

"Hear what?" He rubbed his eyes.

"That strange sound."

He tilted his head to listen, but all he could hear was the storm and the howl of the wind. "What sound?"

"I couldn't tell you exactly. It was weird…like an animal or bird maybe…but loud."

He listened again. "I don't h—"

The sound floated across the water, a bizarre intermittent hooting bark, high and musical. It started as a low whooping sound, then rose sharply in pitch.

"There it is again." She clutched at his leg. "Did you hear it?"

"Y-yes, I did."

"Well, what do you think it is?"

They heard it again.

It made the hair on the back of his neck stand up. It was a peculiar, complex, and amorphous sound. He couldn't put his finger on it. It could've been man-made, an animal, or perhaps even several animals chorusing.

"It's eerie, isn't it?" she said.

He nodded, becoming aware of his own heavy breathing and his quickening pulse. He'd never heard anything like it. It was pained, otherworldly. It came at regular intervals, each whoop followed by a long pause.

They lay awake for hours, listening to the strange sound—and the storm, always the storm.

***

"Son of a sodding whore!" hissed Ron, shouting his rebuke at the rain while steering into the waves. It was before dawn, their progress had slowed to eight knots, they were deep downwind and running dark, but it was a risk he was prepared to take. He'd considered turning her about to the windward and heaving to, but decided against it. *No, better to run. Better to get away. Away from it—whatever it was.*

That's when he heard it again, that same curious, whooping call they'd heard during the night. It sent shivers down his spine.

Oh, Jesus. He breathed heavily, gripping the wheel with white-knuckled hands. Self-doubt threatened to set in.

He tried the line again, but the sail simply refused to trim. The winch retorted with a sharp motorized squeal, while the storm jib fluttered in the gale.

He ground his teeth. *Of all the times and places to experience gear failure. Undone by a simple thing.*

He lashed the wheel and went aft to investigate.

Testing the line, he quickly found the source of the problem: a cheap block with a faulty bushing.

"Damn," he said, and went to the cockpit to grab his tools. Difficult work under the circumstances, but he was able to jury-rig something—he kept one eye on the sea the whole time. Their run-in with the thing had given him the jitters.

He didn't fear the sea; he was accustomed to the elements. The sea could be a cruel mistress, but he was used to her cunning. Nor did he fear the storm so much as the unseen force that moved behind it. It was the presence in the darkness he couldn't understand. He'd felt it nearly all his life, ebbing and flowing in the corners of the world—corrupt and conspiring, exerting its malicious will. It was there on the Mekong Delta, during the endless patrols and firefights. It was there when his buddy, Rallo, was hit, and the tide ran crimson with his blood.

No, I'll be damned if I let it get me.

He finished jury-rigging the storm jib and line, went aft, and unlashed the wheel.

He'd worked through the trauma. His memory of the years in Nam was the splinter his mind couldn't expel. He left Wyoming a nineteen-year-old kid, but came back an animal. He was wired and scared to death of everything. His nerves were all shot to shit, and he jumped at every sound.

Trying the winch again, he trimmed the sail, this time, with ease.

Margaret had been the one to save him. She'd brought him back from the abyss and taught him there was something worth living for.

But now, he recollected, Margaret was below deck, on the master berth, bleeding into their white linen. He'd carried her there. She'd been breathing shallowly; her face was deathly pale, and she vomited blood.

He knew she needed medical attention, and fast, or she wasn't going to make it 'til morning. He'd tried to put pressure on the wound, to stem the bleeding, but the blood had seeped from between his fingers. *She might already be—*

He froze. He heard it again: a high-pitched whoop from out of the dark.

"Go to hell!" he screamed into the eye of the storm. *It must've been following us all this time.*

The whooping came again, only this time it seemed closer.

It's back. He hated it with every fibre of his being.

There came a—*thunk*—from the side of the boat. Ron squinted. He thought he saw movement, but he couldn't be sure.

He lashed the wheel again and went forward, this time brandishing the claw hammer from the toolbox.

Edging closer, he tried to discern the shape in the dark. *Is it there, or is it my imagination?* The thing rose to its full height, a great, looming, hulking mass.

Ron opened his mouth in slack-jawed horror.

He swung the hammer, but the thing was too quick for him. He felt surprise and pain as the thing punctured his belly. His muscles clenched, and the veins stood out on his neck. It lifted him until his feet were off the deck—the whole while he was bleeding and screaming. The shrill sound, foreign to his ears. *It found me,* he thought before he lapsed unconscious. *It found me....*

1

Dr. Martin Buchinsky's office was in Downtown Fort Lauderdale. As therapists go, he was only middle-of-the-road expensive, although you wouldn't know it from looking at his office. Dani removed her scarf and glanced around the room. It was generously appointed with a Persian rug, wood panelling, and open shelving, with rows of books on display. It smelled of cedar and leather upholstery.

Buchinsky sat behind his desk, looking over the top of his glasses at her, his impeccably groomed beard giving him the air of a Greek philosopher.

"I like the fishing boat," Dani said, pointing at the decorative embossing on Buchinsky's antique desk organizer.

He raised an eyebrow, leaning forward to examine it. He chuckled. "Y'know, I never noticed that before? The stylist picked it." He sat back. "But I don't think you've come here to talk about antiques, have you? You've been dancing around the subject for ten minutes. Would you like to tell me what's bothering you?"

Dani fidgeted, wringing her hands and scarf. Her mousy blonde hair framed a pretty face. "I haven't been sleeping."

"More nightmares?"

She nodded.

"Want to walk me through it?"

She looked away.

"I understand it's painful, but it will help to talk about it," he said, removing his eyeglasses.

She bit her lip and sighed. "They start the same way they always do: it's late at night and it's raining. My parents and I are in the car, returning from a family friend's. I'm in the back, dressed in my pajamas, nodding off from listening to the windscreen wipers."

"And how old are you in these dreams?"

She thought for a moment. "Eight."

"I see. Go on." He scribbled a note.

"Mom is wearing this oversized sweater. No makeup, though. She never wore makeup. Dad is smiling. He had a great smile." A tear ran down her face.

Buchinsky offered her a Kleenex from the box on his desk.

She dabbed at her tears. "As I was saying, Mom and Dad were smiling. We started playing the Picnic Game."

"The Picnic Game?" Buchinsky asked.

"You know, it's a car game: one person starts by saying 'I'm going on a picnic, and I'm bringing...' the second person fills in the blank."

Buchinsky nodded.

"Anyways, it's a windy, coastal road, and the surface is slick. Outside, the sea is black and specked with whitecaps. Then we get to the bridge..."

"That's where it happened?" Buchinsky asked.

She nodded. "We're not even halfway across when

14

the semitrailer, approaching us from the opposite direction, crosses the lane lines. Dad lets out a cry, gripping and turning the wheel—we manage to veer out of the way. The car skids, and we smash, careening through the guardrail barrier. For a moment, we are in a free fall, weightless. Then the car hits and we roll down the embankment into the water."

Her hands trembled.

"Dad is knocked unconscious on impact. Mom's awake, although, moving slowly. Her hand goes to the cut on her forehead. She has this look of surprise. 'Mom?' I say, terrified by the water, even then."

She paused.

"We float for a while before the car starts to sink. More and more water flows in. It's cold. It's jarring. I'm trapped, panicked. The water has risen past our waists. I try to move, but I'm held in place by my seat belt."

"And what do you do?" Buchinsky asked.

"I yell for Mom, but the water is past our necks. She looks at me with this expression I'll never forget. I take one last, long breath, then, we're fully submerged. I finally undo my seat belt, turning around so I face the door. I try to force it, but can't manage due to the pressure from the other side. I try kicking at the window, but it doesn't break. It's no good—not with the soft-soled sneakers I'm wearing. My lungs feel ready to burst. Every ounce of me wants to breathe, but if I open my mouth, my lungs will fill with seawater. How long can I hold on? I think, before everything goes to black."

"So, how did you escape the car?" he asked.

"Well, that's the big mystery," Dani said. "I don't know how. I've drawn a blank on this over the years. I woke on a pebbled beach, wet and ragged. Some passers-by found me and called the police, and the police called the coast guard. Divers found my parents' car, upside down, about 20 feet below the surface. And weirdly, the right rear passenger-side door was torn from its hinges."

Buchinsky mused. "And your parents?"

"Drowned," Dani said. "There was an investigation. I went through years of counselling. I stayed with my aunt and uncle."

He took his glasses, put the notebook down, and picked up a stack of envelope-sized cards. "I'm going to show you some images now, and I want you to tell me how they make you feel, okay?"

"Okay," she said, crossing her arms.

"What do you think when you see this one?" He held up the first card.

It was a fairly innocuous picture of a child in a swimming pool, wearing a pair of pastel-colored floaties.

Dani cleared her throat. Her heart beat faster and she broke out in a sweat. "I know I shouldn't feel this way, but I do. It's an odd sensation, chilling."

"Uh-huh. And what about this one?" he said, showing her another card.

It was a picture of several women sunbathing on a beach.

"How does it make you feel?"

Dani hyperventilated, and the room spun.

"Okay, let's stop there. "Let's bring it back. Take a breath." He put away the cards.

Dani did her best to collect herself.

He went and poured her a glass of water from the pitcher on the side table. "Here," he said, handing it to her. "Take as much time as you need."

"Thanks," she said, taking a few careful sips. "Is

that what you expected to happen?"

"Not exactly," he said. "This was instructive, nonetheless."

"Instructive?"

He nodded and sat back down. "I want to talk now about the incident from the other day. What happened? I want to hear it back again, if you don't mind? So, I can get the details."

Dani sighed.

"You were driving home from the mall?" he said, prompting her.

She nodded. "I was in heavy traffic, with the shopping on the back seat. It was a hot day, and I was worried the heat might spoil the groceries. I had the a/c all the way up."

"You said you had some kind of reaction?"

"I came to a bridge on Sunrise Blvd, caught sight of the beach, and started shaking."

"When you saw the ocean?"

"Uh-huh—I mean, what the fuck is that?"

He shifted in his chair. "It sounds like you had a panic attack."

She frowned.

"Did you try the breathing exercise like we talked about: breathe in deep through the nose, count to ten, then exhale for another count of ten?"

"It didn't work."

"You have to give it a chance, Dani," he said. "You tried it, and that's the first step—so good for you. You are going to get through this okay. It's a process. Thalassophobia is no laughing matter."

Dani rubbed the back of her neck.

"It's not uncommon for people to fear the sea," he said. "We should all have a healthy respect for the sea.

It's a normal ancestral trait. We are programmed through evolution to fear: extreme heights, snakes, and…deep water. It's a primal fear. Humans are land mammals and, therefore, unsuited to harsh marine environments. We all fear the dark in some form or another. It just so happens you fear the ocean."

"I mean…I live near water," she said. "Our house backs onto the bay. It was never a problem until now."

"Until the nightmares?"

She nodded.

"So, the question is—what are you truly afraid of? What do you think is going to happen?"

"I don't know," she said. "I can't seem to shake this feeling of impending doom."

He maintained steady eye contact. "A lot of people fear the ocean, Dani, but your fear is an *irrational* fear, and this is what we need to address in these sessions. Thalassophobia can be connected to a traumatic event in the past: the loss of your parents, in your case."

She rubbed at her eyes, trying to hide the redness.

"And how is your husband through all of this?

"Chip?" she said. "I haven't told him."

"Why not?"

She coughed. "I don't think he'll be supportive. It's just…I don't want to worry him."

"I think you should tell him, don't you?"

She shrugged. "Are you going to give me some pills for this, Doc?"

Buchinsky opened his drawer, retrieving what looked like a small writing pad. "I'm going to give you a prescription for Prozac? It's proven to be effective in the treatment of anxiety. It should help you to sleep." He tore off the page and handed it to her, his hand brushing hers.

"Thanks, Doc," she said.

"You'll need to take it twice daily. The directions are on there.

She got up to go.

"And how's the painting?" he asked.

"Good. Very relaxing."

"Well, keep it up." He hugged her. "A painting of the sea, a walk on the beach, it all counts as exposure therapy to help you deal with your phobia. It's a process, okay? We'll get you there."

2

It was a mild and sunny morning. Detective Sgt. Frank Hagen stepped out of an unmarked patrol car, donned his shades, and crossed the street. He walked with a slight limp, with his hands in his pockets, and head down. He sipped on coffee from a takeaway cup. His gun and badge were visible around the folds of his suit jacket. He stopped and waited for a couple of cars to pass before stepping onto the curb. The Blue Jay nightclub was a popular nightspot on Broward Boulevard. However, in the daytime, the neon sign, mounted high on the dark brick wall above the club, looked strange and out of place.

He shifted his focus to the alley next to the club. Police had cordoned off a section of the sidewalk. The forensics van was already there.

Frank ducked under the police tape. A uniformed officer looked like he was about to say something, but Frank flashed his badge, and the way parted like the Red Sea for Moses.

The alley was strewn with crinkled trash bags and food scraps from the restaurant next door. The back door and windows of the club were barred. Wooden pallets and a moldy-old-mattress were stacked against a metal fire-escape.

Crime scene investigators wearing forensic gloves picked through rubbish, looking for evidence, making sure to leave markers if they found anything. The crime scene photographer took photos—*click, click, click.* Meanwhile, the victim was sprawled out, dead, next to the dumpster.

Frank thought it was an animal carcass at first—it was so badly mutilated. The woman had large crescent-shaped bloody marks on her neck and arms, and her face was all torn up. He saw her yellow dress, stained with blood, and his gut tightened. A kaleidoscope of images flashed through his mind, and a part of him snapped free, drifting back, back to a year earlier…

You're breathing heavily while running up the stairs to a house in the middle of nowhere. There's been a radio call. A drug dealer lives here—a stone-cold killer by the name of Ramírez. You get to the door, and your heart is pounding. Adrenaline pumping. All colors seem bright, details stark and brilliant.

"Police. Open up!" you say.

No answer.

You've already radioed for backup, but you can't wait. He's abducted a girl. It'll take too long you decide, so, with gun drawn, you kick in the door.

Moving rapidly down the hall, you scan and clear each of the rooms of danger, like you were trained. All your senses are heightened. In the living room and kitchen, there's broken crockery on the floor. There's a trail of blood, and you think, 'how strange,' as there are peas and carrots all through the carpet.

"Police!" you say again. "Come out where I can

see you."

You're moving quicker now, up the stairs to the bedrooms. You check each room, but when you get to the final room, you smell a coppery smell, like coins. It's the girl's blood. She's pale and her stomach's been cut open, its contents spilled on the floor. She's wearing a blood-splattered yellow dress. You start to hyperventilate. The windows aren't open. Bile rises in your throat. You hear a sound. BANG! A gunshot. An explosion of pain in your leg, as—

"Frank? Earth to Frank. Are you okay?"

"Huh," Frank said, snapping back to the present. A familiar figure stood before him. "Oh, hey, Manny."

Emmanuel Dusola was a homicide detective, and a darn good one. Not as good as Frank, of course, but damn near close.

"Are you okay, mi amigo? You looked out of it for a second."

"Yeah, I'm fine." He rubbed his eyes, then sipped his coffee. Frank knelt beside the body. He grunted, ignoring the dull ache in his thigh. "Sweet Jesus. What have we got here?" He scrunched his tie and held it over his nose. The body had started to decompose, and flies were buzzing.

"Some Jane Doe. No ID. The manager of the club called it in," Manny said. "One of the servers found her here, next to the dumpster, this morning, when they put out the trash. 24 hours, do you think?"

"At least," Frank said. "What happened to her face?"

"Bite marks," Manny said.

"Damn. That's the second one this month."

"Con~o," Manny said, the frustration evident in

his voice. "That's ri-ight, there was that jogger, too. What was her name again?"

"Mandy James, 31. She was stabbed and bitten at Esplanade Park."

"If you ask me, hoss—given her proximity to the club—this is probably an overdose. Maybe a stray dog or dumpster rats had a chew postmortem, y'know?"

"Maybe. A little farfetched, don't you think?"

Manny shrugged.

"Heck of a way to go, though. Nobody deserves to go like this." Frank took a pen from his lapel pocket and used it to gently lift and examine the gold necklace around the victim's lacerated neck. The necklace was intricate, with pearl inlays. It was unlike anything he'd seen before. "With a piece of bling like that we can rule out robbery. What do you think?"

Manny whistled in appreciation.

"Have you spoken to the Manager? Do we know if the girl was a customer?" Frank asked.

"Si, señor," Manny said sarcastically. "He can't recognize her."

"What about camera footage? They must have CCTV?"

"Nada. Their security is pretty lax. Their cameras are out of order—due for an upgrade next week."

Frank rolled his eyes.

"He gave us the name and phone number for the bouncer," Manny said, "who was on duty the last couple of nights. There's a good chance that *if* she were a customer, this guy would remember."

"Sounds like a lead."

"I've been calling, but no answer. You know what these nightshift guys are like. He's probably asleep."

"Well, let me know if you get hold of him. Maybe

we'll catch a break. He might've seen her come in with somebody."

Frank looked at the bite marks on the victim's face again and swore under his breath. "—the fuck?"

"You're telling me, hoss."

3

"Hey, Albert," Dani said, as she entered the diner.

Albert beamed. "Dani!" He stood by the espresso machine, tapping out the used coffee grounds. "Just the employee I wanted to see."

There was a murmur of voices, laughter, and the clinking of spoons. A queue of customers stood by waiting for their orders. The Sunrise Diner was your typical waterside Fort Lauderdale café, frequented by a mix of both locals and tourists.

Albert used the milk frother, with a squeal and a scrape of metal. As the proprietor, he liked being where the action was, up front and talking to the customers.

"Why, what's up?" She gave him a peck on the cheek. He was a burly guy with a beak-like nose and a goofy expression.

"It's Friday. Which means it's busy."

"Uh-huh," Dani said, still feeling the lingering effects after her therapy session. Albert continued talking as she ducked around the corner to a storage closet, which had a row of shelves that doubled as staff lockers. She stowed her handbag and went to remove her scarf, but it wasn't there. *Dammit.* She took a blister pack of pills from her handbag—the ones that Buchinsky prescribed—and swallowed one down.

She returned to the serving area while putting on an apron. Beth had arrived and was sitting at one of the bar stools. She was medium height, with freckles, and wavy brown hair.

Dani smiled.

Beth removed her baker boy hat and gave her hair a tussle.

A waiter passed them and tripped—*Whoah!*—and Beth coolly sidestepped, narrowly getting missed by projectile food and drinks.

SMASH!

"Godammit," Albert said. "Can someone please clean that?"

Dani looked at Beth with wide eyes. "Honestly, I don't know how you do that."

Beth shrugged. "Just lucky, I guess," touching cheeks.

They had been friends for as long as Dani could remember. Beth was down-to-earth and loyal to a fault. She was a regular fixture at the diner, seeing she worked around the corner at BCE Bank.

"D'ya hear what I said?" Albert interjected.

"Oh, sorry, hon. "You said it was busy?"

Albert rolled his eyes. "No, after that." He tapped out another lot of coffee grounds. "Mindy's called in sick, and I need someone to cover her tables."

Dani mused. "I can do it."

Albert raised an eyebrow. "Are you sure? It's outside. Remember what happened the last time?"

"I'll be fine," Dani said.

"Great! At least that's sorted," Albert said. "Say, did I tell you a customer complimented your paintings today?"

"Really?" Dani said. She'd been doing artwork on the side and aspired to become a full-time artist. Albert couldn't have been more supportive and encouraged her to hang them in the diner.

The kitchen doors swung open, and the chef set down a tray with several plates.

"You're up," Albert said. "Can you take care of that order?"

Dani saluted and made her way outside.

The outdoor area overlooked the waters of the bay; its reflective surface shimmering, as a catamaran glided past, sailing along with the outflowing tide.

What am I afraid of?

A family sat at one of the tables: a mother, father, and their young son.

"Who ordered the crispy chicken burger?" Dani asked. She could feel beads of sweat forming on her brow. She imagined herself floating, sinking.

"I did," said the kid.

Dani set the plate down.

"And the shrimp salad?"

Dani looked again, mesmerized by the catamaran. She thought of the bay and the city's arterial system of canals, all flowing to the Atlantic. *'It's not uncommon for people to fear the sea,'* she remembered Buchinsky saying. *'We all fear the dark in some form or another.'*

Suddenly, she felt dizzy and had difficulty breathing.

"Everything okay, Miss?" the Dad asked.

She saw stars in front of her eyes and felt herself collapsing. A moment later, there was a loud— *CRASH*—and everything faded to dark.

When Dani regained consciousness, she was sprawled on the tiles amid a mess of broken crockery and French fries. Beth and Albert wore worried expressions—Albert's usual goofy expression was replaced with a genuine look of concern.

A small crowd had gathered. The other customers in the diner watched on curiously. A pugnacious-looking man, who sat at the table closest, leered.

"Help you?" Beth said, indignantly.

He harrumphed and went back to eating his breakfast burrito.

"Beth squeezed Dani's shoulders.

Dani blinked. "Wh-what happened?"

"You blacked out."

She sat up. "Sorry, I-I don't know what—"

"You okay?" Albert asked. "Can you stand?"

Dani stood, shakily.

"Woah—easy now." Beth supported her by the elbow. The crowd had dispersed.

"Sorry, Albert, that's twice today," referring to the broken plates.

"Don't worry. I'm sorry I suggested it when you weren't ready. Do you need to take the day?"

Dani shook her head.

Albert looked at her askance. "Well, take a breather at least? Let me know if you need anything," leaving Dani and Beth alone.

They sat at an inside table, a short while later. Dani shut her eyes and counted down, slowly, before saying, "Jeez, that was embarrassing."

"Don't worry about it," Beth said. "They probably see shit like that all the time."

"You think so?"

"No," chortled Beth. "What was that, epilepsy?"

"I'll tell you, but you have to promise not to laugh."

Beth frowned.

Dani considered. "I have a phobia of water. It's called thalassophobia."

"You've never said anything about it before?"

"I didn't have it before. I sort of developed it."

"But you live in Lauderdale."

Dani shrugged. "The fainting and anxiety attacks don't happen often. Albert's been pretty good about it, considering. He lets me cover the inside tables."

"So, what does that mean, you can't go to the beach or swimming?"

"Nope. All of that's off bounds for a while."

Beth looked down. "Have you seen a therapist?"

"I have…I mean…I am. He says it stems from the accident, when I was a kid, y'know?"

"Of course." Beth frowned. "Jeez, I'm sorry, Dani."

"What for? You didn't have anything to do with it."

Beth put her hand on Dani's. "Are you getting enough sleep? You look tired."

"It's the humidity plus these bad dreams I've been having."

"Dreams?"

Dani nodded. "Last night, I dreamed I was back in that car again, drowning. It felt real."

"It's understandable considering what you've been through," Beth said. "I have bad dreams all the time. Not quite what you're talking about, though. I have one where my teeth fall out."

Dani gave a meek smile.

"Hey, what's your star sign?" Beth said, changing the subject. She took a newspaper from the adjacent table.

"Gemini. Why?"

"I'm guessing you haven't had your horoscope read in a while?"

Dani shook her head.

Beth flicked through the pages till she found the relevant section. (reading) "Gemini…You've been feeling restless, but you're finally getting the chance to discern what matters most...Mercury is in retrograde." (skipping ahead) "Ah-ha—here now this is interesting. Watch out for the unexpected. Romance abounds." She waggled her eyebrows.

Beth's eyes darted from side to side, presumably as she read her own horoscope. "I prefer yours," she said, putting the paper down.

"By the way, you're not going to believe who I saw yesterday?" Beth said, changing the subject again.

"Who?"

"Hannah MacGuire."

"God. Really?"

"She's had work done and looks like a human parade float."

They laughed.

Albert came to the table with a couple of blueberry muffins. "Here you are. On the house!"

"Naw—thank you," Beth said, in a hokey singsong voice.

Albert retreated to the espresso bar.

"That was nice," Dani said, tearing off a piece.

Beth chuckled. "He's probably worried you're going to sue him for the fall."

Dani rolled her eyes. "He's not like that."

"How's Nate?" Dani asked.

"Oh, that fucktrumpet," Beth said, rolling her eyes. "We broke up."

"That's sad. I kinda liked Nate."

"Yeah, well. I'm seeing a new guy now: Matteo. He's in a band. And you? How's Chip?" Beth asked.

"Don't even ask."

"That bad, huh?"

"He's got a problem. He spends all his time on betting apps—when he's not at the gym, staring at his own reflection."

Beth snorted.

"He's been playing poker and losing. When I confront him about the missing funds, he gets angry. It's affecting our relationship."

"Gambling's an addiction, babe—as bad as heroin or any other drug."

"He's talking about going to Miami with his friends."

"Are you worried he's going to cheat on you?"

Dani's eyes filled with tears. "Well, I wasn't until now."

Beth put a hand on her friend's shoulder. "Have you thought of staging an intervention? He could go to Gam-anon?"

"Are you kidding? He'd pitch a fit."

4

"Hey, Dani, there's a guy who wants to buy one of your paintings?" Albert said.

"Oh, really? Which one?" Dani said, setting down a plate of key lime pie—once Beth had left, she'd settled into the rhythms of a typical workday.

"I don't sell them, I just hang them," Albert grinned. "Go talk to him."

She looked in that direction. The man sat at one of the tables with his laptop open.

The stranger was tall, handsome, about thirty-five years old, with slicked-back hair, dressed in jeans and a sports jacket.

"So, you're the painter?" he said, speaking with a low, resonant voice. He took a sip from a glass of water on the table.

"That's right," she said. He had dark, deep brown eyes. They were black, the color of onyx—the kind you could get lost in for days. Her heart skipped a beat; a strange feeling of excitement and unease crept over her.

He looked at the wall where several of her paintings were hanging. He had high cheekbones, a strong jaw, and the most exquisite eyebrows Dani had ever seen. "They're good. You've got talent," nodding appreciatively.

"You flatter me," she said, "Mister—?"

"Gilman. Eric Gilman." He offered his hand.

Dani shook it, realizing her ring was absent from her ring finger. *I must have left it at home, on the soap dish above the sink.*

He looked at her, and all other distractions, people, and noise, faded. It was as if there was only the stranger and the light in his eyes, glinting like starlight against a devouring night. *Something about him seemed so familiar.*

"Sorry, have we met before?"

"No, I don't think so. I think I would have remembered. I'm not from around here. I'm merely passing through."

"Oh, and are you interested in art, Mr. Gilman?"

"Call me Eric." He flashed a smile. "You could say that—I'm an art dealer."

"You're kidding?" She raised an eyebrow. *Could this be my chance?* Butterflies fluttered in her belly. She bit her lip to prevent herself from giving an excited squeal. "What's that like?"

"It has its moments." He took another sip of water.

Underneath his handsome exterior, she sensed a sadness, a melancholy, which she couldn't put her finger on.

"Albert said you want to buy one of my paintings?"

He nodded. "This one," and walked over to the painting—one of her seascapes.

"It's excellent. You've captured the mood and the light perfectly. It's a standout work. Really. Art like this will get you noticed."

Dani blushed.

"How much is it?" he asked.

"The price tag says $250," Dani shrugged, "but it's negotiable."

"The price is fine." He handed her the cash.

Dani couldn't believe it. She'd only sold a handful of paintings before, and never for the full asking price. "Would you like it wrapped?"

"Sure." He closed his laptop and finished his water.

Dani took the painting from the wall and went to the counter.

While wrapping it, in bubble wrap and brown paper, she noticed Eric watching her. *What's his deal?* His focus made her self-conscious, yet, at the same time, it thrilled her.

"Where'd you learn to paint?" he asked.

"I'm self-taught. I used to paint urban scenes: buildings, parks, and people on streets. But this painting is different. It's special. It was my first seascape. Now, all I do is seascapes."

"Well, I'm honored," he said. "It's clear it means a lot to you."

"They all do, I guess."

"Do you want to be a painter full time?"

"You could say that," she said, still wrapping. "That's the goal. Working here is a means to an end— until I can make it as a full-time, professional artist. It's my dream."

"It's a nice dream." He smiled. "Will it bring you happiness?"

Dani tilted her head. "Nobody's ever asked me that before…Yes. I think so."

"And do you have family? What does your

boyfriend think?"

Dani's stomach tensed. *Where is this line of questioning going?*

"I'm married."

"Happily?" he asked, making eye contact.

"Oh, you're trouble," she smirked, finishing with the wrapping. "You're not trying to seduce me, are you, Eric?"

"Well, that depends," he said.

"On?"

"Whether it's working?"

Dani laughed despite herself.

"Listen, I want you to have this," he said, handing her his business card. "From time to time—if an artist is talented enough—I'll represent them. To serve as an intermediary between the artist and potential buyers. You know, help them promote their work…secure exhibitions?"

Dani's eyes widened. There *was* an attraction there. It was undeniable. And now this handsome stranger was offering her an opportunity, a leg up as an artist.

"Call me," he said.

"I don't think I can. Like I said, I'm a married woman." She glanced to the side, conscious someone might be watching.

"A life too quiet is a dead sea," he said. "It's more pleasant when there are two."

"That's an odd expression."

"Not especially," he said. "Anyway…It was nice meeting you, Dani."

"Nice meeting you, too," she said, shaking his hand, dazed.

When he left, she felt like she'd been in a deep sleep, as if driving on autopilot.

5

You're back in the car again. Floating in darkness. Fully immersed. Your lungs are spasming, but you need to preserve oxygen. It's cold, your eyes are open, but it's blurry under the water. Sinking fast. Panic. Your heart is pounding...

Awake. Dani's eyes snapped open. She turned over, propped herself on her elbow; the digital display of the alarm clock read 7:00 am. She hit the button to end the beeping and sank back onto the mattress, expelling a moan. Her head was reeling. It took her a while to get centered, still shaken from the effects of her dream.

She reached but found the other half of the bed vacant. *Chip must be up already.* In a pedal wheel motion, she kicked the sheets into a knot at the foot of the bed. A sliver of light shone through the threadbare curtains of their bedroom, illuminating a cloud of floating dust particles. *Jesus. It's only 7 am, and already it feels like the inside of an oven.*

Dani got out of bed, spread her toes on the carpet, and yawned. Looking at her reflection in the closet mirror, she pinched her belly. She wore an old t-shirt and underwear, revealing a pair of naturally toned legs.

She thought about Eric Gilman, the handsome art dealer she'd met the previous day. Tall, charming, sophisticated, he had an air of mystery, an enigmatic quality. Yet there was something about him that seemed familiar. It was a feeling more than anything else, a feeling she couldn't place.

It meant a lot to her that he'd bought one of her paintings. *At least someone is interested.* She took his business card from a drawer and ran a thumb across the embossed lettering.

He'd offered to represent her. *Was that just a line?* He'd flirted with her—it was blatant. *I'd be lying if I said I wasn't flattered.* That voice, and those dark brown eyes—they stirred feelings in her. He exuded power, a sense of danger, and it excited her.

Maybe I should call him? It was dangerous to think in this way. *Can he really help promote my art?*

"I can't." She put the card back in the drawer. To see the man again would be too much of a temptation. She wasn't ready to give up on her relationship with Chip. *I owe it to myself to make my marriage work.* She didn't think she could lie to Chip anyway. She wasn't a good liar and wouldn't cope with the sneaking around. Still, a part of her wanted to see Eric again.

Downstairs, in the kitchen, she filled a bowl with oatmeal before fetching milk from the fridge. She shut the fridge door to reveal Chip standing there.

Dani squealed and cuffed him on the shoulder. "Don't scare me like that."

"You're looking bright-eyed and bushy-tailed," he said, jogging on the spot, before doing a few half-hearted star jumps. He was neatly dressed in runners, a polo shirt, and shorts—standard attire for a SweatFit employee.

Chip was medium height, with an athletic build and a strong jaw. He'd played football in college, but dropped out to become a personal trainer. Repetition's essential to every workout, he was fond of saying. That's why he made a good trainer, because of his stubbornness, his pig-headedness. That was also why they were together: he'd pestered her until she finally agreed to go out with him.

"I thought you were at the diner today?"

"I'm going in later," she said, mixing milk into her oatmeal.

Picking up a knife, he chopped a few ingredients and dropped them into the blender, hitting the button.

"What are you making?" she asked, wincing at the high-pitched squeal of the blades. It was like he was trying to aggravate her.

"Huh?" he said.

"What—are—you—making?"

"Juice cleanser." He stopped the blender and poured the greenish mixture into a glass. "You want some?"

Dani crinkled her nose. "No thanks." Last time she'd had one of his health shakes, she nearly soiled herself. It didn't help that he never followed a recipe.

"Suit yourself." He drank, flexing a well-muscled, tribal-tattoo-covered arm before letting out a satisfied sound. "This is *the shit*, though."

Dani ate her oatmeal. She wondered what he'd done with the cash he'd borrowed the previous week. *He's blown it already, probably.*

"I had one of my clients cancel on me this morning," he said. "I told the lady I needed 24 hours' notice. She thought I was being too harsh. 'Whatever.' I said, 'We all have things come up. I still need the notice.'"

Dani agreed. "So, I sold one of my paintings yesterday."

"Augh, no!" exclaimed Chip, patting his chest in frustration.

"What? What's the matter?" she asked.

"I got shake on me," he huffed.

"Come here." She drew him to the sink and dabbed at the offending spot with a damp cloth.

Chip gave her a look.

"What?" she said.

"Nothing. Just…you know…you look after me." He grinned.

"There you are. See? All gone."

"Thanks, babe."

She went to kiss him, but he failed to notice.

"Remember me saying we should get a Jet Ski?" he said, changing the subject.

"Huh?" Dani scowled. "I thought you gave up that idea. I remember saying it was too expensive."

Chip looked hurt. "I found a pretty good deal, though."

Dani put her hands on her hips. "I'm against it, babe. We can't afford it. They're a waste of money."

He tilted his head. "I think you're overreacting."

"I'm not sure I am," Dani said. "It's not just the cost of the Jet Ski, it's the insurance, and the maintenance…Need I go on?"

"Shit, is that the time?" he said, checking his imaginary wristwatch. "I better go."

"Babe?" she said, following him as he blazed a trail for the door. He snatched his gym bag as he went.

"I'll see you tonight," he said, propping the screen door open.

She nodded, then added, "Don't get that Jet Ski."

The screen door banged shut.

Chip nearly stumbled at the broken step at the foot of the porch.

"I thought you were going to fix that?" she called after him.

"I am," he called back, unlocking the SUV.

Dani waited until he'd backed out of the drive and disappeared up the street.

Gone. Dang, it's hot. She looked at her overgrown lawn, partially shaded by the enormous Palm tree. She'd liked the little tree-lined street when they'd first moved to Dorland Park. The cicadas buzzed. She closed the door. The quiet was deafening.

6

Nestled amidst a string of uniform homes, on a narrow street in Flagler Heights, stood a dingy, weatherboard house with a low-pitched roof, peeling paint, and rusted gutters. Frank Hagen sat across the street in the passenger seat of an unmarked police car. He observed the house, then checked the side-view mirror. The street was deserted except for a few kids playing on a rope swing, under a tangled oak tree. He adjusted the A/C vents, redirecting the flow of air.

"So, what did he do?" asked the uniformed officer behind the wheel.

"Huh?" Frank said, still watching the house.

"Arlo—the perp. What did he do?"

Frank held back a grin. *Did Barnes just say perp, like an extra on CSI: Miami?* "He tortured and killed some guy—sent body parts to the widow courtesy of the U.S. Postal Service."

Barnes grimaced. "Why?"

"Turf thing. The victim was a rival gang member."

Barnes swallowed. "How did we know it was him?"

"I've got a CI in there, Zeke, one of Arlo's buddies

42

who's turned snitch in return for a reduction in his charges."

"Right," Barnes said, nodding.

"C'mon, kid." Frank bumped him with his elbow. "Time to get your game face on."

Frank's sunglasses fogged immediately as they stepped from the car. The sun beat down, and the cicadas were shrilling.

Holy Toledo, it's hot. He removed his jacket.

"What's the plan?" Barnes asked.

"No plan. We go knock on the front door? The sooner we cuff him, the sooner we're outta here."

They crossed the street and started up the driveway. The kids on the swing watched them with curiosity, then ran off.

The curtain in the front window of the house moved.

"Well, it looks like someone's home," Frank said, drawing his gun from his hip holster.

Barnes did the same.

A moment later, the fly screen popped off the house's side window, and two figures jumped out.

Frank exchanged a glance with Barnes, and they quickened their pace.

"POLICE! FREEZE!"

Arlo stumbled on the grass, a big guy with a wife-beater shirt, and tattoos on his chest and arms—hate symbols denoting his gang status.

Zeke stood behind, a low-slung redneck with a dim-witted expression.

"I said freeze! Get your hands up!"

Zeke raised his hands while Arlo stood slowly. He glanced over his shoulder then back again.

"Don't!" yelled Frank.

Arlo bolted. Zeke looked at Frank, swallowed, then ran off, too. They disappeared behind a cinder block wall. Frank had to refrain from shooting because of the close confines between houses.

"Don't just stand there," Frank said to Barnes. "Circle round back."

Barnes nodded before hightailing it back in the direction of the car.

Frank chased after the escaping felons, rounding the corner in time to see them climbing the neighbor's timber fence.

"Shit," Frank said, holstering his gun. He readied himself but fumbled it on the first attempt. Searing pain. His old leg injury made it difficult to leap over. He tried again and made it, landing on the other side with a jarring thud.

It took a moment to get his bearings. The yard was thirty by forty feet, roughly, with a clothesline running down its center. *Movement.* A soft cotton dress fluttered in the breeze. He glimpsed Arlo as he ducked behind a line of washing.

Frank followed, with gun drawn, but collided with the woman who a moment before had been hanging out her washing.

"Hey!" she yelled.

"Sorry," called back Frank, still running.

Arlo and Zeke looked back before scaling the next fence.

Seeing the fence, Frank thought, *Fuck it,* put his head down, readied his shoulder, and barged through. He found himself in the alley on the other side, rotten timbers and all. He could hear the felons' echoey footfalls.

They're getting away. Frank puffed still in pursuit.

They had widened the gap and were nearing the end of the alley. Arlo looked back and grinned, just as Barnes pulled up in the patrol car in front of him, slamming the brakes. Unable to stop their forward motion, Arlo and Zeke bounced off the side.

"Turn around!" yelled Frank.

Enraged, Arlo threw a punch. Frank dodged and struck the man under the chin with his open palm, simultaneously sweeping his leg. The heavy man dropped like a sack of potatoes.

Arlo went to get up.

"Stay down," Frank yelled.

"Don't shoot," Zeke pleaded, his hands raised.

"You got 'em?" Barnes said, stepping from the car, a hint of admiration in his voice.

"Cuff these shitbags, please?" Frank said. "And read them their rights."

"With pleasure," Barnes said. "You have the right to remain silent," he began.

"Why'd the hell you run?" Frank said to Zeke.

He shrugged. "It seemed like a good idea at the time."

Frank rolled his eyes.

A fierce-looking dog barked from where it was chained in a neighboring yard.

"Anything you say will be used against you in a court of law," Barnes continued.

"I'm innocent," Arlo said. "I didn't do nuthin'."

Bark, bark, bark—went the dog.

"I don't know, Arlo," Frank said. "Do you always vacate your domicile via a window? I call that suspicious behavior."

Barnes snickered.

"Fuck you, Pig," Arlo hissed. "Do you even have a

warrant?"

"Oh, you best believe I've got a warrant for your sorry ass," Frank said.

The neighbor with the dog came into the yard to investigate the commotion. He was wearing a dressing gown and was having a general snoop.

"Sir, I'm sorry, but can you please take your dog inside?" Barnes asked.

The man shrugged. "Rambo doesn't like Five-O."

Frank chuckled.

Once Arlo and Zeke were safely detained in the back seat of the patrol car, Barnes breathed a sigh of relief. Arlo glowered at him through the window.

If looks could kill. "Well done, kid," Frank said.

Barnes grinned and got back in the driver's seat.

Frank went to get in when his cell phone rang.

"Sergeant Hagen," he answered.

"Hey, Frank," the voice said. It was Dusola.

Frank signalled Barnes to wait and closed the passenger-side door. "Hey, Manny. What's up?"

"I've got something you're gonna want to hear."

"Lay it on me," Frank said, bemused.

"We got a positive ID on dumpster girl."

Frank raised his eyebrows. "How?"

"Some mighty fine police work on my part, I don't mind saying. I spoke with the bouncer from the Blue Jay. He said he remembered seeing a girl from two nights ago who matched the description of our Jane Doe."

"She was wearing a yellow dress?" Frank asked.

"Si," Manny said. "Anyway, it turns out she'd started a bar tab, and get this…she'd left her credit card behind the bar. Plus, she never came back for it."

"Yeah, well, now we know why," Frank said. "So,

who is she?"

"Harris, Melissa. 23," Manny said (reading).

"Uh-huh. Do we know anything about her?"

"Not really. Not yet. We're looking into her background. The bouncer remembered something else, though."

"Oh yeah, what was that?"

"She *wasn't* alone. She sat in one of the booths, talking to some dude for most of the night."

"Did you get a description of said dude?"

"Nope. Unfortunately. It gets pretty dark in the club, so he never got a good look at him."

"Hmm. Typical."

"You want me to call you if I find out anything else?"

"Si, mi amigo. Nice work."

Dusola laughed. "De nada."

7

Dani stood in the downstairs bedroom of their Dorland Park home—a room she'd repurposed as her art studio. It was late, and Chip was asleep. Dani liked to paint at night. It allowed her easy access to her muse. Everything was still and quiet, the only sounds the susurration of the breeze in the leaves of the tree outside her window, and the muted sounds of traffic.

When Dani first took up painting, years earlier, she'd used watercolours, or gouache, before graduating to oil paints. She preferred the medium. The colors were so much more vibrant, and the textures were at another level.

Her first paintings had been of people: local landscapes, landmarks, people commuting, and mothers with their children at the park. She would paint from photos or memory. Dani only switched to painting seascapes at Buchinsky's urging. She'd been resistant at first, concerned about what memories she might awaken.

She decided this next piece would be a seascape, a night scene. She started with a rough sketch on an artist's pad using an HB pencil to get a feel for the general composition. She had a photo of Central Beach as a reference. Taking her palette and paint knife, she mixed the colors—making sure to add linseed oil to slow the drying time—black for the sky, navy and green for the ocean, raw umber for the rocks and sand.

Placing the stretched canvas on the easel, she took a deep breath, put in her earphones, and hit play. This was Dani's nightly ritual, her meditation. David Bowie's *Slow Burn* was first on the playlist. The world slowly dissolved, and she experienced a sort of expansion, a trance-like state.

Using a flat brush, she blocked in the sky, the horizon, and the beach in the foreground, switching to a round brush when it became necessary to gently blend the colors. She used her knife to add detail to the rocks, scratching fine lines in the wet paint. A dry brush was used to add shadow or soften edges. Layer after successive layer was added, creating a textured look.

Moving faster and faster, her muse took over, her brushstrokes smooth and effortless. Now and then, she would reference her pencil sketch to make sure the composition was on track. The painting began to come together. Deep inside, something told her this painting was different, different from anything she'd ever painted.

Buchinsky would have called the act of painting therapy. Although Dani felt it was more like exorcising demons—her twin demons: sorrow and loss. She'd take all her memories of the past, all her pent-up feelings, and express them onto the canvas, a literal pouring out of her soul.

Using a lighter tint, she added the effects of the surging of the waves, the crests, the breakers, and the foam. Water was always difficult. Dani understood that when it came to water, it was the light from above that made all the difference. So, with the tip of her finger, she added the moon as the light source, and suddenly the piece sprang to life—a wistful and gloomy nocturne.

In that moment, it was as if she had fallen through the canvas into the private world of her painting. It was a weird middle-place where dream and reality overlapped. She had flashes of memory, which in this place seemed real: a half-drowned child on a beach; her parents' car, submerged and sinking fast. Suddenly, she felt as if she were drowning.

With her paintbrush, she expressed all her pain, all her loss, her desire for love. It was like a door had opened, a door to a forgotten part of herself. The painting was so life-like, she fancied she could hear the sound of the ocean, the rolling of the waves, the ebb and flow of the tides, the rumble of thunder. She could smell the sea air. It was at once exciting and frightening.

When the painting was done, Dani stood back from the easel, exhausted, spent. She was happy with her work, but taking a closer look felt something was missing. Considering for a moment, she took her paintbrush and added a lone figure, a woman in a gossamer-like dress. She looked beyond the breakers, as if waiting. For what?

The inclusion of this was surprising. Dani hadn't planned it as part of the composition, but seeing her on the canvas felt right. She knew this was an expression of herself, her ideal self. Strong. Unafraid. Maybe it was part of the process, part of the exposure therapy Buchinsky kept talking about. Dani glanced at the clock on the wall and realized she'd lost track of time. She had to go to bed.

Before turning out the light, she took a last look at the painting, with its storm clouds, the tumult of the waves, the woman standing steadfast in the shore break. It gave her hope.

8

Mrs. Werner winced. It was hot, and the canvas tote bag she carried—full of groceries—was pressing into her shoulder. *This will teach me to go shopping when I'm hungry.*

Toby, her silky Maltese terrier, sniffed the sidewalk, looked at her, and wagged his tail.

"You're a good boy," Werner muttered.

The farmers' market was part of their weekly ritual. Toby had his daily walk, and she enjoyed shopping at the various street stalls for fresh produce, knick-knacks, and sweet-smelling soaps. She'd stopped at Café Bien for beignets.

Werner was a small woman with gray hair. She had turned 75 in May, but who was counting? She wore a navy-and-white-striped tee-shirt, capri pants, and a comfortable pair of flats for walking. She made a point of walking everywhere.

Toby darted excitedly left and right.

"Almost home, Toby," she said. *The key to staying young is to avoid stagnation.* Before she was an artist, she'd been a nurse and knew the effects of premature aging on people who sat around and did nothing. She was determined to keep moving.

They turned the corner onto their tree-lined street. She liked the neighborhood. It was peaceful, leafy.

Werner stopped in the shade of a tree to catch her breath. She could see her house, a solid little single-story number her husband, Earl, had built nearly fifty years earlier. It was in the mid-century modern style, stuccoed, and painted a delightful turquoise. She loved it dearly.

The sound of cicadas buzzed in her ears. She leaned against the tree for support. Toby looked at her briefly before going back to sniffing the verge.

Beads of sweat formed on her brow. She frowned. The heartburn was back.

She looked at her garden and at how tall the grass had become. *It's all this rain we've been having. That's okay. Javier will be by later to cut it.* She didn't mow the lawn herself anymore—doctor's orders. The grass used to be cut regularly. When Earl was alive, the garden was his domain. Aaron, her son, had tried for a while—back when he used to visit.

She looked at the neighbor's place. Their garden was just as overgrown. A lawn sprinkler came on, and Toby barked at a pigeon. Werner pulled the leash.

"Easy, Toby." She led him across the street. "You wouldn't know what to do with him even if you caught him."

***

Inside, she set her keys on the hall table, where various framed photos of family and friends were arranged. It was noticeably cooler inside than out.

"Who wants a treat?" she said to Toby.

He looked at her expectantly.

Inside, on the way to the kitchen, she walked past her studio, cluttered with paints, canvas, and drying brushes. Setting the tote bag and groceries on the breakfast nook, she put the coffee pot on to boil and gave Toby his treat. He trotted across the linoleum and out the doggy flap in the rear door.

Removing the pastry box from the groceries, she took a bite of a beignet and eyed the wall-mounted telephone. It was the kind with an old curly cord—as unintentionally retro as the rest of the kitchen. There was an emptiness in the pit of her stomach. Aaron and his wife, Sarah, were in Ohio—so far away, it may as well have been the moon. *Why don't you call him?* She looked again at the telephone.

Her mouth went dry, and she set aside the beignet. *Why did he have to go and accept that management position?* She thought back to several years earlier. *Their visits had been infrequent, but at least I got to see my granddaughter. She'd be a young woman now, almost nineteen.* She sighed.

I know! I'll call and speak with Sarah, woman to woman. She has to understand...what it's been like: first losing Earl, the man I loved for forty years; then, gradually, losing Aaron. Who am I kidding? She's too young and stubborn to understand.

She resisted the urge to call Aaron. Instead, she poured herself coffee. *You had to make a thing of it, didn't you?* She thought back to the argument, but banished the unpleasant memory.

I should paint. That'll get my mind off it.

The doggy door flapped, signaling Toby's return. He lay at her feet, and she patted him. For a moment, the emptiness melted away.

9

"How was your day?" Dani asked, setting the steaming dish on the table.

"What, babe?" Chip said, positioning himself for a better view of the TV. The Dolphins were playing the New York Jets, and they were getting thrashed. "Goddammit. That was holding. C'mon, ref, are you blind? I've got money on this."

"I said, how was your day?"

"Um, good," dialing in the volume with the remote. "Are you fuckin' kidding me? Another commercial break?" He threw the remote on the table. "What is this?"

"Meatloaf," Dani said.

Chip loaded his fork, shoveling an obscene amount of food into his mouth. "Needs salt?" he said, when he finally stopped chewing. "It's a little bland."

Dani passed the salt. There was an awkward pause.

"You're quiet."

Dani was caught off guard, and her food went down the wrong way. She coughed. "Sorry. Am I?"

He shrugged. "You're usually full of small talk and news. I'm lucky if I can get a word in edgewise, usually."

Dani grimaced. "Sorry I—"

"Finally!" Chip said, talking at the TV. "Now, don't lateral it. Pull it in close. Hold the ball!"

Dani went back to her food.

"You pick up my dry cleaning today?" Chip asked, using the table as an elbow rest, sawing at his food with his knife.

"No, sorry, I forgot."

Chip frowned. "So, what *did* you do all day?"

"Clean, mostly."

"I ran into Dora Phillips at the gym," Chip said.

"Oh? And what did she say?"

"Well, her son, Dumpy—do you remember him?"

"Oh, you mean, Brad."

"Right, Dumpy Brad Phillips—apparently, he's practicing law now and he's bought himself a Tesla, can you believe it?"

"Really?" Dani said, appreciatively. "Good for him."

"Yeah, good for Dumpy," Chip said. "I bet he sucked a lot of dick at that law firm to pay for that prissy streetbeater."

Dani frowned. "You don't have to be envious, babe. You're doing pretty well, considering."

"Envious of that little twerp? Forget about it," he said, shoveling food into an already overstuffed mouth.

"So, have you thought anymore about us starting the savings plan?" Dani asked, wanting to change the subject.

"What for?" Chip tilted his head.

"You know," Dani said, looking at her hands. "We spoke about being prepared for an emergency...peace of mind. To avoid living outside our means."

"I can't remember agreeing to that."

"We spoke about it. A savings plan would be good." Dani swallowed.

Chip shook his head. "I already told Martin, at work, I'd invest three grand into his car washing business."

"That's not what we discussed, Chip. We said we'd start a savings plan. Some of that money is mine."

"I don't think you understand, babe. This is an opportunity to get in at the ground level with a startup. A new venture! That's big bucks."

"One in five businesses fail in their first year, Chip. It's risky." Dani said. "And you hardly know Martin. He's been there for...what...five months?"

"Is this a dig at me? I think you could be more supportive."

"Supportive? I'm nothing but supportive, Chip, but you chew through money like it's going out of style.

"Where do you get this crap?" Chip said, chuckling. "I mean, grow up, Dani. It's an investment. Honestly, I expected more from you. This just shows how askew your priorities are. So selfish."

"Selfish?" Dani said, indignantly.

"Easy," Chip said, trying to diffuse things.

"No, I won't go easy." Dani stood, her chair skidding backwards. "You're the one behaving like a juvenile."

"Don't raise your voice to me," Chip said, slamming his palm on the table.

Dani squeezed her fists tight until her fingernails dug deep into her palms, and her face flushed hot. *You hateful asshole.* She saw the defiant gleam in Chip's eye, and her lower lip quivered. Hot tears blurred her vision, and she left the room.

10

Dani was surprised when Jane, the owner of Vanguard Galleries, telephoned. She was a VIP in the art world, a real mover and shaker. Not much was said on the phone. Dani secretly hoped it might be her big break.

She fidgeted.

The waiting room was arranged in the mid-century modern style with high vaulted ceilings and dark wood panelling. The artwork of several local artists adorned the walls, some of which Dani recognized. There was a selection of Pippa Moore's portraits, highly balanced compositions featuring A-list celebrities, sports personas, and inspirational figures. There were also some of Jacquie Owen's works, a delightful blend of surrealism and Art Nouveau.

Nearby, a glass water cooler gurgled, and the air conditioning droned overhead.

On the wall opposite was a painting by Helen Werner, an artist whom Dani much admired. Werner was a veritable titan in the local scene, known for her striking seascapes. This one depicted a quiet little bay area, with boats at anchor. Dani marvelled at the artist's tiny brush strokes.

The effect Werner had achieved in the reflective surface of the water was nothing short of astonishing, and the longer Dani observed, the more the painting drew her in. It made her think back to the first time she, herself, painted a seascape: the chemical smell of the paint, her brush darting across the canvas, the ebb and flow of the waves. She could almost hear the rumble of the ocean and feel the sand beneath her feet.

"Danielle?" a voice said.

"Yes?"

"I'm Jane Brennan," the woman said, offering her hand. "Simply marvellous to meet you."

Jane wore her black hair in a short bob. She was tall and chic; was in her sixties, but could pass for a late forties; and wore an elegant figure-hugging dress.

"Nice to meet you, too," Dani said, taken aback. She was surprised by the woman's warmth, considering she had a reputation as a bit of a shark.

"This is my receptionist, Olivia."

The woman nodded.

"Hello," Dani said.

"Oh, well. Come, come," Jane said, gesturing for Dani to follow. "There's much for us to talk about."

The inside of Jane's office was as lavish as the reception area: there was a Murano glass vase on the sideboard, a Hockney painting behind her desk, and an oversized designer rug on the floor.

"Please, sit." Jane gestured. "Coffee?"

Dani thought about it. "Sure. If you're having one?"

Jane nodded. "Olivia, can you bring in coffee?" she said over the intercom.

"I suppose you're wondering why I asked you here

today?" Jane smiled, forming her hands into a steeple.

"The thought did cross my mind. Is it about a job?"

Jane let out a delightful, bell-like laugh. "A job? Oh, now, that's fabulous. No, not a job per se. Do you know Eric Gilman?"

Dani blinked. "Arr, yes. We only just met."

"Well, he knows you, darling," Jane said. "He's an art dealer—with impeccable taste, by the way. I don't know the man personally. He's very mysterious. He's worked with galleries from LA to DC and New York. So, I trust his eye. He's recommended you. He sees your talent."

Dani sighed. "I'll take that as a compliment."

"So you should, darling. Now, I have an offer for you," she continued. "If you'll hear me out?

"Recently—on Mr. Gilman's advice, and through an assistant—I managed to obtain an original of yours…a seascape. It has a woman, in the foreground, staring out to sea."

"You bought that?"

Jane nodded, then waved her hand dismissively. "I was suitably impressed. I looked at more of your work online. I think you're talented. Very *now*."

Dani blushed. It was one thing for friends to say they liked her art, but for Jane Brennan, a true art connoisseur, to pay her a compliment was another thing entirely. Suddenly, she felt validated, *seen*.

"Wow, thanks, Ms. Brennan," Dani said.

"Oh, please, darling, call me Jane."

"Jane then," Dani said.

At that moment, Olivia entered with their coffee on a tray.

Dani accepted hers.

"Yes, well, I think the subject matter," Jane continued, "the sombre mood of your pieces is simply excellent. I think it's the vulnerability of the female figure in the foreground, contrasted with the ruggedness of the seaside rocks, the sand, and waves. Excellent."

Dani grinned.

"I'd like to see more of your work," Jane said. "How many pieces would you say you have?"

Dani considered the question. "In storage? I'd say around forty."

Jane's eyes widened. "Fabulous. Get them out of storage. I'd like to exhibit your work here at the gallery. Are you interested?"

Dani couldn't believe her ears. She sat forward. "Of course."

"Good. I'll have my assistant draw up the contract. It's a standard contract. You'll earn fifty per cent on any pieces sold. The other fifty goes to the gallery. We've got to be able to pay to advertise, pay the rent, and keep the lights on."

Dani took a deep breath. *This could change everything. Maybe I won't have to work at the café anymore.* "I appreciate this, Jane. It's very generous."

"Only too happy to do it, darling. I recognize talent when I see it. You'll have to thank Mr. Gilman, too, for the referral."

11

Dani was at the local Stop & Shop, gliding between the aisles while balancing her weight on the cold metal of the shopping cart. Easy-listening music played in the background, accented by the electronic bleeps from checkouts.

She pushed past a towering end display, piled high with soup cans. Boxes of colorful cereal lined the cream-painted shelving. She had the entire week's grocery budget burning a hole in her pocket, but she'd left the shopping list at home. *Shoot.*

Her body was full of tension. Maybe she was due for a spa day or a massage. It had been months since she'd been laid—what with Chip always being out. He wasn't interested anymore. Perhaps this was a good thing? Buchinsky would have called it an opportunity for personal growth. *'People who chose to be celibate were often more mindful or self-aware,'* he said.

She passed the bakery aisle and was greeted with the comforting aroma of freshly baked bread.

Fluorescent lights shone overhead, and a banner read, *"Welcome. Organic Produce."* Brightly covered fruit and vegetables adorned the display stands.

She passed a man dressed like Gordon Gecko having an animated conversation on his cell.

"I don't care what Thompson thinks he can get us, Hudson and Kirlin can get us twice…"

A stressed mother was trying to console her whining toddler, who was bawling their eyes out over not being allowed candy.

Dani scooted past, careful not to make eye contact. This was her quiet time, her meditation. She had a headache and popped a couple of Prozac, downing them without water.

A Bowie song chimed in over the store speakers, "Young Americans." When she was sure no one was looking, she did a little dance, shifting her weight from foot to foot. *If anyone saw me right now, I'd just about die.* No sooner had she thought this she saw a familiar face.

She stopped. It was Eric—her *mystery man.* He was at the end of the aisle, but he hadn't seen her yet. She felt a combination of excitement, nervousness, and attraction. There were butterflies in her stomach, and her heart raced. She swallowed. *Oh, god. He'll think I'm stalking—*

He turned and waved.

She pretended she didn't see him. Picking up a cantaloupe, she pressed it with her thumb and sniffed it to check its ripeness.

"Fancy meeting you here," he said.

"Oh, hey," she said. "Eric isn't it?"

"That's right." He smiled.

Dani watched him. His eyes were softly lit, dark, and infinite. Then, she realized, he watched her, too.

She coughed. "Do you shop here often?"

"Not really. I happened to be passing and thought I'd give it a try—Y'know…I do believe the cantaloupes are in season now."

Her cheeks reddened. "$3.10 apiece," she said, putting the cantaloupe back.

They walked the aisle and perused the stands together. Dani felt cool air over her skin, as they passed the meat counter, and she shivered.

"I owe you some thanks," she said.

"Oh? What for?"

"For referring me to Vanguard Galleries."

"So, you got the call? Good."

"Jane Brennan said you made the introduction?"

"I did."

She pursed her lips, calculating what she might say next. "But why?"

He chuckled. "Isn't it what you wanted?"

"I'm not used to people doing nice things for me."

He waved this off. "It was nothing. I was glad to help."

"They're going to exhibit my work, y'know?"

"That's great. You deserve it. You're very talented."

"Thanks," she said, blushing. She swept her hair behind her ear. "I don't think I need to tell you what a big deal this is. How can I repay you?"

"Let me buy you dinner?"

She froze, hardly able to believe her ears. He *was* flirting with her. "We hardly know each other."

"I was hoping we might change that."

Dani took a box from his cart. It was cake mix. "Devil's food cake?"

He shrugged. "I have a sweet tooth. So, sue me."

"I'm no saint either."

They looked into each other's eyes. He was handsome. She was drawn to him, and had to remind herself they were in a public place.

"Raincheck?" she said.

12

The white-tiled examination room was buried two stories deep in the basement of the Medical Examiner's Office. It smelled of ammonia and bleach, and was uncomfortably cold. One side of the room was lined with stainless steel coolers, cabinets where the bodies were stored.

"Sorry to bother you, Brian," Frank said. The fluorescent light flickered overhead. It gave Frank the jitters.

"No bother," said the portly pathologist, dressed in navy blue scrubs and a lab coat. He had the misfortune of having the last name Crawley, so naturally, they called him Creepy behind his back at the station house. Under his hairnet, he had a noticeable comb-over. He removed his surgical mask and gloves, washing his hands at the sink. "To tell you the truth...I'm glad for the interruption. We don't get many visitors here." After drying off, he extended a hand for Frank to shake.

There was a moment's pause. *I wonder how many cadavers he's touched this morning,* thought Frank, before shaking. "Yeah, well, this one's a strange one, so I wanted to come and speak with you in person anyway."

"Uh-huh—I'm glad you did," Brian said. "Follow me."

They walked to one end of the room—the sound of their shuffling, rubber-soled shoes echoing off the tiled floor—where a body-shaped mound lay under a sheet on the examination table. Brian removed the sheet, without ceremony, revealing the naked and mangled body of Melissa Harris.

Frank was hit with the unmistakable smell of decomposition and decay. He covered his nose instinctively.

"I don't know how you do it, Brian."

"Huh? What's that?"

"The smell. How do you deal with it?"

Brian laughed. "You stop noticing it after a while. Here," he said, taking something from a drawer and handing it to Frank. "It's Vicks rub. You dab it under your nose."

"I remember. No thanks."

"You sure? It'll help with the smell."

Frank grimaced, then followed the man's advice.

It's different seeing her lying there, a slab of meat with a toe tag. His eyes went to the adjoining tray table, covered in an array of sterile tools: scalpels, scissors, forceps...a saw. He tasted acid, swallowing hard to fight back the nausea. Her body was as pale and bloodless as he remembered, except this time, there was an ugly "Y" shaped incision starting at the shoulders and extending down to the pubic bone, held together with large stitches. There were similar stitches across the forehead, too, where the scalp had been sewn back on.

Brian went and sat on a stool over by the counter,

unwrapped a sandwich from a brown paper bag, and took a large bite. "Sorry," he said, mouth stuffed full of food. "You don't mind, do you? You've caught me on my break."

"Knock yourself out," Frank said, his stomach doing somersaults. The Vicks didn't seem to be working; it only helped to open his sinuses. He coughed. *There's that acid taste again.* Looking the body over, he again saw the bite marks to her face and the lacerations on her neck. *The wounds are terrible.*

"Jesus," Frank said, shaking his head. "Nobody deserves to go like this."

Brian chuckled, took another bite of his sandwich, and swallowed. "Yeah, well, nobody 'goes' quite like her...except for that jogger woman they brought in earlier this month."

Frank raised his eyebrows. "You mean Mandy James. The stabbing victim."

"Uh-huh," said Brian.

"What was the same? You mean the bites."

"Yes, the bites...but, not just the bites." The insides fell out of his sandwich and onto the counter. He picked through the pieces before popping a mayonnaise-covered pickle in his mouth. He further punctuated this unsanitary display by licking each of his fingers clean, in turn. "For this one, rigor mortis and lividity were consistent with the estimated time of death, but...as for the manner of her death...She was a tough one to figure. You could say she gave me the *cold shoulder*."

Frank rolled his eyes.

Brian grinned. "Tough crowd. That one usually *kills*."

Frank interjected. "We were under the assumption

maybe dumpster dogs chewed on her body…after she died, y'know?"

"I don't think so," Brian said. "Firstly, canis lupus familiaris, your average dog, leaves a pretty distinctive bite mark. Nope, this was something else."

"What?"

Brian shrugged. "Hard to say. Some of the bite marks look…almost human."

"Shit. So, first Mandy James, and now this one? Are you saying we have a biter on our hands?"

Brian raised his hand. "Hold your horses. I said *almost*. The other marks are in a weird, crescent-shaped, cut or puncture pattern, left by unusually sharp teeth."

"You think the unsub was maybe wearing some falsies, dentures?"

"Don't know. But, here's something I do know…those bites—same as the other girl—happened antemortem—as in before they died."

"—the fuck?"

Brian took another bite of his sandwich.

"Are you sure?"

"Positive." He tried to swallow. "Cutting into live tissue always causes a different reaction than cutting into dead tissue. For one, there's usually bleeding, and for two, antemortem injuries typically contain a chemical, leukotriene B4, a chemical involved in inflammation."

Frank took a moment to absorb this information.

"And, it gets weirder," Brian said.

Frank ran a hand through his hair. "Gets weirder, how?"

"Here, take a look at this," Brian said, standing. "There's a puncture wound about one inch below the sternum." He pointed.

Frank leaned in. "You think that's what killed her?"

"Yes and no," Brian said. "What killed her was the massive amount of animal venom in her system."

"Animal venom?! Are you serious?"

"I'm *dead* serious, Frank." Brian grinned. "In all my years as a Medical examiner—and I've seen some shit—this takes the cake."

"How do you mean?"

Brian pointed again. "Take a look. You can see evidence of trauma, massive amounts of swelling, and tissue damage around the wound."

Frank leaned in for a closer look. "You do a tox screen?"

Brian took a clipboard and flipped through the pages of the report until he came to the right section. "Ahah! Here it is. I wrote it down (reading) 'consistent with cyastins, peroxiredoxin, and galectin.' These types of venom are usually found in marine animal stings."

"—the fuck?" Frank said.

"The fuck is right," Brian said. "I've never seen anything like it."

13

The bullpen was a section of office space at Fort Lauderdale's Police Department, set aside specifically for detectives' use—so named for its correlation to its baseball equivalent, where the major players warmed up before a game. It was where detectives exchanged ideas, discussed cases, and followed up on leads. It was a veritable boys' club, a font of testosterone. It had rows of desks and computers. There was the constant whir of printers, phones ringing, and the murmur of dispatchers speaking into headsets coming from the next room. It smelled musty, a combination of metal and sweat. The bullpen was in the thoroughfare, people moving busily, back and forth, from room to room, without much regard for the work taking place. It was in some ways the beating heart of the FLPD operation.

"So, how was Creepy?" Manny asked.

Frank poured himself coffee from a carafe on the side. Framed photos of police officers in uniform and Rotary Club plaques lined the walls. He left out the cream when he realised it had curdled. "You know...same old creepy," he said, sitting. He removed his jacket and loosened his tie.

"C'mon, spill. Did you find anything?"

Frank sipped his coffee and glanced at the case files stacked in his in-tray. "I did." And he proceeded to tell Manny about his findings at the Medical Examiner's office.

"Coño," Manny said under his breath. "This is whacked out, crazy. Have you ever seen anything like this before?"

"Nope. Never."

"So, we're looking for a vampire, or a dude wearing false teeth, who injects his victims with animal venom?"

"Uh-huh. Although I doubt he's a vampire. Not in The Sunshine State."

They laughed.

There was a commotion. Some plain clothes led an uncooperative suspect, in handcuffs, to be processed. A glum-looking man with frazzled hair. They led him past the interrogation rooms, towards detention.

"Hey Frank," said one of the plain clothes.

It was Barnes.

"Oh, hey, Kid."

"Carjacker," Barnes said, laughing. "Genius, here, thought he'd make a quick getaway. Too bad he can't drive a stick."

The man swore, but then Barnes applied pressure to his shoulder and arm, which made him give a high-pitched squeal. Everyone within earshot laughed.

When they were gone, Frank turned to see Manny leaning back in his chair, with a contented look on his face.

"So, you wanna tell me why you're so pleased with yourself?" Frank took another sip of coffee.

Manny clasped his hands behind his head. "I just got back from Melissa Harris's apartment."

"You serious?" Frank said, raising his eyebrows. "Why didn't you say so before? How did you swing that?"

"Permission from the parents. The building superintendent let us in." He shrugged.

Frank sat forward. "Let me guess…you found something?"

Manny nodded. "Uh-huh. She had a laptop. So, I gave it to Linus in Computer Forensics, you know, to do a sweep. Then we did the same for that previous victim, Mandy James' laptop—and do you know what we found?"

Frank shrugged.

"It turns out Harris and James worked pretty long hours, lived on their own, and they both belonged to the Miss Lonely Heart Club, y'know?—figuratively speaking."

"You want to maybe speed this up, Sherlock?"

"Alright. Hold your horses. Anyways, it turns out they both used a dating website called Date Swift— where the date is spelled with a D and an 8, get it?"

"Got it. Clever."

"Well, it turns out Harris—a.k.a. ShyBabe123— had a date that night with someone using the handle, Proteus."

"Proteus?" Frank scratched his head. "What's that? Latin?"

Manny Shrugged. "It turns out James had a date with this Proteus character, too. What do you think, this Proteus guy could be the unsub?"

"Definitely. Sounds like a good candidate. Can we

get the website to release the deets?"

"I already thought of that, but the users are completely anonymous. Linus said the site is overseas and encrypted."

Frank swore.

"I know. I can't even tell you...To think there is a psycho out there preying on these lonely girls."

Frank snaps his fingers. "I've got an idea. You wanna know how we catch this guy?"

"How?" Manny said.

"We set up our own profile—a fake profile—with the handle...I dunno...LoverGirl69 or something."

Manny laughed.

"We set up the profile and we go hunting for this...this Proteus," Frank said.

"The hunter becomes the hunted, eh?"

"Exactly."

14

Helen Werner stood in the reception area of The Vanguard Galleries.

"Helen, darling! What a pleasant surprise," Jane Brennan said.

"I happened to be in the neighbourhood," Helen said, with a smile. "I had my royalties check to collect." She brandished the slip of paper before stowing it in her tote bag.

"Can you stay for lunch?"

Helen shook her head. "Maybe another time?"

"Sure. A little notice next time, though, okay? I'll have Olivia make a reservation at Bartleby's."

"Have you been working much?"

"Some. I'm working on a medium-sized piece now—a sunset, on a beach, with a blue ocean. It might be my best work yet."

"Fantastic!" Jane said. "I want to see it. You'll have to bring it with you next time."

Helen nodded.

"Jane, there was another reason I came in today. I wanted to get your thoughts on something."

"Oh?"

"What would you say about an exhibition of my latest work in the fall?"

Jane's cheeks flushed with color. "Ah, to be honest, I've already given that spot to someone else."

"Oh?" Helen said, looking down at her feet. "To who?"

"Honestly, I didn't think you were working much anymore, otherwise—"

Helen raised her hand in a quieting gesture. "Who did you give it to?"

Jane shrugged. "A young up-and-comer, Dani Kowalski. You wouldn't know her."

Helen shook her head.

Jane put a hand on Helen's shoulder. "I've already promised Dani the spot; otherwise I would…"

Helen folded her arms.

"We can show your work at the same time next year." Jane coughed. "Would you like that?"

Helen pursed her lips.

Changing the subject, Jane asked, "Do you have anything else planned for today?"

"No, nothing else," Helen said, looking into the middle distance. "Hey, here's an idea? Why don't you drop this young nobody?"

Jane stepped back. "I'm shocked you would even make the suggestion."

Helen shrugged. "Whatever happened to looking after your best clients first?"

Jane grimaced. "You know I'm an advocate for self-promotion, darling, but you take it too far. You're not seriously suggesting I drop Miss Kowalski and show your work, instead?"

"That's exactly what I'm suggesting." Helen

planted her feet wider. "Or, would you prefer I show my work to the *Campbell Art Gallery* in Miami?"

"Now, darling," Jane said, blinking, "let's not make any hasty decisions. I'll need time to mull this over. I mean...the ink's not even dry on Kowalski's contract. I'll have to figure out a way to break the news."

"I'm sure you'll work it out."

15

Dani and Eric walked together beside the bay, passing the time pleasantly, locked in conversation. The water rippled, boats swayed at anchor, and puffy, white clouds scudded across the sky. She stopped by the railing and looked forlornly out to sea. The tide was coming in.

"What's wrong?" Eric asked.

"Oh, I'm being silly," she said, sniffed, and wiped away a tear. "It's embarrassing. I don't want to burden you."

"Dani," he said, putting a hand on her shoulder. "If something's bothering you, you can tell me."

She smiled. "Thank you, Eric. I don't even know how to explain. I'm feeling a little overwhelmed."

"What is it?"

She sighed. "I lost the exhibition slot."

"What? How?" Eric said, taken aback.

"Helen Werner got it instead. She must have talked Jane into it. Star power, y'know?

Eric's face reddened. "She has no right—"

"What's done is done. No use crying over spilled milk," she said, frowning. "I'm just sad. Especially seeing you went to the trouble of making the

80

introduction. It would have been a great opportunity."

Eric crossed his arms. "Spilled milk? You're right. Don't worry about it. Life has a way of righting the wrongs. I'm sure if you're patient, another opportunity will come along."

"Thanks, Eric," she smiled. "I appreciate your support," and started crying again.

"What?" he said, touching her arm. "You're not telling me everything, are you?"

"No. It's Chip…he…"

Eric tilted his head. "What about him? Has he hurt you?"

"No, god no, nothing like that. He has a gambling problem. He's bet, and lost, a lot of our savings, and keeps buying things we can't afford. I don't know what to do."

Eric clenched his fists, but quickly regained his composure. "Don't worry. Everything's going to be okay. You'll see."

***

Dani felt a droplet of rain on the back of her hand. The puffy clouds were replaced with darker ones. There came the low rumble of thunder, the sky opened, and it lashed down with sheets of rain. She let out an awkward squeal, and they dashed for the cover of a nearby ficus tree.

"Where did this come from?" Dani said, taking the shortened umbrella from her handbag.

Eric was already drenched. She felt sorry for him and invited him to share her umbrella, but soon regretted it, realizing she had to raise it to an uncomfortable height.

"Thanks," Eric said. "I don't think it's going to let up."

Dani agreed, trying not to feel self-conscious while pressed against him, the warmth of his body noticeable through their soaked clothes. Dani mused at the odd set of creases on his neck. *Funny. I haven't noticed them before.* She glanced at his lips and wondered what it would be like to kiss them.

"Which way are you headed?" Eric asked.

"I'm parked over that way." Dani pointed. "You?"

Eric pointed in the opposite direction, "I live about two blocks over."

There was an awkward pause.

"I can walk with you," Dani blurted out.

Eric waved this off. "I wouldn't ask—"

"Don't be silly. I'm not going to drive off and leave you to walk home in this. I'm not going to just give you my umbrella either." She pulled a funny face.

"Fair enough. Shall we go?" He offered her the crook of his arm.

She smirked. "We shall," accepting it. And they broke cover. They kept their heads down while navigating the puddles on the sidewalk.

"Where are we going?" she asked, after a while, for it seemed like they were moving away from the residential area.

"I told you…" and he nodded in the direction of the bay.

Dani looked blankly at Eric, then in the direction he gestured. All she saw were a series of floating piers and yachts. "You live on a boat?" She felt a flutter of nervousness.

"I'll show you," he said.

At the marina, they walked past the dockmaster's office, and down a gangway. The sound of the lapping water made her dizzy, and she had difficulty breathing.

"You okay?" Eric asked.

She felt a hot flash, her vision narrowed, and she started to fall. Eric caught her.

"What was that?" he said. "You fainted?"

"I'm sorry." Her cheeks flushed. "I have a phobia of water. It frightens me."

"Really?" He said, intrigued. "Don't worry. Open your mind. You're with me," and he took her hand.

Miraculously, she felt a wave of confidence. His touch seemed to dispel her fear. She did her best to keep pace while holding the umbrella.

They passed a row of pristine sailboats, the rain disturbing the water's surface, making a gentle hissing sound. She felt woozy, but nothing like the fear she'd felt earlier.

"This is it," he said, stopping in front of a pretty, sailing yacht. "She's a 42-footer."

Dani gasped, "It's beautiful." It was dark green with a gold leaf stripe, and luxurious hardwood coaming. "How can you—"

"Afford it?" He laughed. "That's okay, you can ask. Art dealing can be a lucrative trade—if you know what you're doing. You find the right client...an exceptional art piece...and make a sale. Do that a few times and you start to amass a fortune."

"The *Halcyon Daze*?" Dani said, noting the name scrolled across the bow.

Eric grinned. "Cute, huh? I sailed her here from Seattle. I'll keep dealing in art till I've saved enough to sail around the world, permanently."

"Well, it sounds wonderful." She shivered, realizing she'd allowed herself to get cold.

"Oh shoot. Where are my manners? Would you like to come aboard? Maybe dry off and wait for the rain to stop?"

Dani gulped. Walking along the pier was one thing, but going aboard… *Do I dare? What if I faint?* It was a handsome-looking boat, and she didn't relish the idea of walking back to the car. "Sure. Okay." Her reservations dissolved with the rain.

"Good," Eric said, leaping with catlike grace onto the gunwale. "Come on up." He offered his hand.

Dani bit her lip and considered the distance. *I'm crazy for doing this.* She felt imbued with an inner confidence she hadn't felt in a long while. She shook out her umbrella and tucked it into her handbag before reaching to take Eric's hand. "Okay, I'm ready. Permission to come aboard, Captain?"

Eric hoisted her as she leaped, surprising Dani with his physical strength.

She couldn't believe it. *I'm aboard a boat?* None of the usual *dark* thoughts crept in. Eric seemed to have a calming effect on her.

It was surprisingly spacious below deck. The lavish wooden floors were varnished and polished to a high gloss. There was a table, where Eric kept his laptop, and a lounge.

"Wait here," Eric said, going aft, returning a moment later with a fluffy white towel, a pullover with a loose weave, and an enormous pair of tracksuit pants. "They mightn't fit you right, but you can roll up the pant legs."

"That's fine, thanks," Dani said, drying her hair with the towel. "So where can I...?" looking for somewhere private to change.

He showed her to the head.

It was cramped inside the tiny space. There was a faucet and a shower, but little else. She wriggled out of her wet top and bra, drying herself quickly before throwing on the dry clothes.

"Who are you, and what have you done with Dani Kuwolski?" she asked, her reflection in the mirror. She was being rash, impulsive. She felt a pang of guilt as she thought of Chip. *I should have gone back to the car.*

"Do you feel better?" Eric asked, when she returned to the main living area.

Dani was surprised to see him standing, shirtless, in the galley, himself in the process of changing.

"Much better, thank you."

He slipped on a dry tee-shirt. "Would you like a hot drink?" referring to a saucepan he had simmering on the stove.

"Sure. Smells great."

"Hot chocolate," he said, pouring the steaming mixture into a mug.

She sipped at it while the rain pattered on the butterfly hatch, in the ceiling.

"So, tell me about this sailing trip around the world? Where do you think you'll go first?"

"The Florida Keys," he said. "Key West via Key Largo and Marathon."

"Amazing. I always wanted to go, but I don't think I will now."

"Never say never. You may still get your chance." He smiled.

"I hope so."

Eric took the mug from her and set it on the counter. "Close your eyes."

"Why?" she said, managing only a semblance of schoolgirl-like innocence.

"Trust me."

She thought about it then closed her eyes.

He leaned in and kissed her. She was taken aback. It felt good but strange. It had been a long time since she'd kissed anyone but Chip.

Sensing her uncertainty, Eric hesitated. Dani slipped her hands around his neck and they kissed again, deeply. Hurriedly, he reached and drew the pullover from over her head, revealing her nakedness. She gasped as he teased her with his mouth.

"I want you," Eric whispered.

Breathless, Dani agreed.

16

You're back in the car again, floating in darkness, fully immersed, your lungs spasming. You need to preserve oxygen. It's cold. Your eyes are open, but it's blurry under the water. Sinking fast. Panic. Your heart is pounding. You manage to free yourself from your seatbelt. Turning to face the door, you try to force it, but it won't give. You kick at the window, but it doesn't break. Feeling faint now. Incoherent thoughts, racing. Is this the end? Oh, god. So little breath left. Just about ready to pass out. Suddenly, the door wrenches off its hinges and disappears into the deep. Out of the darkness, a webbed, clawed hand reaches in and...

Dani awoke, her heartbeat racing, and her skin was clammy. The room was cramped and dark except for a thin sliver of daylight peaking through the curtains. Her cell phone vibrated on the nightstand, the alarm emitting a familiar electronic chirping. The time read 7:01 AM.

She swung out of bed. *What a disturbing dream.* The feeling of imminent danger and helplessness had been so real. She felt drained, exhausted. Was her subconscious trying to tell her something? Each dream was more vivid than the next. So detailed. Buchinsky would have called it a symptom of past trauma.

Crossing to the bathroom, she splashed water on her face. Her mind went to the previous night. She'd been with Eric. They'd made love. It was hot. Romantic. She felt a shiver of pleasure to think about it—his arms wrapped about her.

Dani wiped her face with the towel and looked at her reflection in the mirror. *Idiot. Why'd you have to sleep with him? You're a married woman.* In her heart of hearts, she knew why. It had been the novelty. Out of boredom. It had been so long since Chip had paid her any mind. When Eric made overtures, it had been a relief. She found him irresistible—those dark eyes. It was raw sexual desire. He'd taken her. They held hands as they made love, her continuous orgasms going off like fireworks.

Maybe *it was* because of her past, her low self-esteem. Growing up without her Mom and Dad meant she had a constant hunger to be loved. She'd just lost the exhibition slot. She wanted to be held. To be kissed. To feel Eric's breath on her skin.

What is it about Eric that makes him so irresistible? Oh, god. Am I falling for him?

Downstairs, she helped herself to coffee from the pot.

"You got in late last night," a voice said.

Dani's stomach lurched. It was Chip. Did he already suspect something? She racked her brain for what to say. "Huh?" she said, casually.

Chip stood in the doorway wearing a polo shirt and

shorts again, munching on toast. "I said you got in late yesterday."

She sipped her coffee. "I met with Beth, but the Honda had a blow-out on the way home. I had to call Triple-A."

"Oh, wow. What a pain," he said.

"It was," Dani said.

"It's a good thing I renewed our membership."

Chip looked at his phone. "Hey, get this…You're not going to believe it. Yesterday, a customer at the gym was doing pull-ups and was using a 100-pound band. In the middle of the workout, the band slipped off the back of his leg and slapped him right in the nuts. He fell on his back yelling, 'MY DICK! MY DICK!'" He laughed. "It was hilarious."

Dani looked out the window at the trees swaying. It was going to be another hot day. "Can I ask you a question?"

Chip put his phone away. "Sounds serious?"

"I checked our bank balance. I noticed money was missing. How much did you take?"

"Jeez, I knew this was coming," Chip said, pinching the bridge of his nose. "Just a few grand."

"Chip!" Dani shook her head. "Do you have any idea how many tables I had to wait—"

"I'll pay it back." Chip shrugged.

"What did you spend it on?"

He looked down at his feet. "A deposit on that Jet Ski."

Dani huffed. "Are you serious? I told you to forget about that thing."

He shrugged. "Look, you don't understand. I got a great deal, okay? It was highway robbery. It was practically begging me to buy it."

"Maybe I'm partly to blame," Dani said. "If I checked the bank balance more often—"

"Look, I don't know what to say. I'm sorry, okay? All I meant was—"

"I'm so exhausted. All the borrowed money and time on those apps. I think you need help, Chip. Gambling addiction is no joke. I shouldn't have to constantly monitor you. Maybe you should join Gam-Anon. If you value this marriage—"

"Gah, this is bull crap," Chip said. "I'll give you this: you really know how to make a big deal out of something. I don't need help. I can stop whenever I want."

Dani raised an eyebrow. "Maybe you're not hearing me. If you love me, you'll see someone. It's important to me."

He laughed, checking his phone, ignoring her.

"It's not funny. I'm really angry this time, Chip." She gave him a simmering look.

"Listen, I don't have time for this right now." He kissed her and darted out the door.

17

Towing a shiny new Jet Ski behind his SUV, Chip lowered the visor to keep the glare from his eyes and pulled into the empty car park at Colohatchee Boat Ramp. Chip would normally be running a client through their paces at that hour, but one had cancelled, and he'd decided to take the morning for himself.

He eyed the Jet Ski, reflected in the rear-view mirror, with a sense of pride. Reversing down the boat ramp, stopping when the ski trailer was half-submerged.

He launched the ski in knee-deep, crystal-clear water, taking it up to the sand. *Fucking Dani. I can't believe she wanted me to take you back to the dealership.*

After parking, he applied sunscreen and thought about all the times Dani had nagged him over the years. *Quit smoking. Put the toilet seat down.* He ground his teeth. *I mean, get off my nuts.*

He flexed his muscled arms at a couple of beach babes who wandered past. He smiled, and they giggled.

They were stunning, he thought, jumping on the Jet Ski. *Not like Dani. Man, she can be ugly when she's angry.* He inserted the key and pressed the start button.

The Jet Ski's engine sprang to life, purring like a kitten.

It was a beautiful morning in Fort Lauderdale. Blue sky. Green water. *It wasn't like this in the beginning.* He pulled back on the throttle and sped out of the cove. Dani caught his eye while on a bar crawl with friends. She'd been this hot twenty-two-year-old, blonde, with pale blue eyes, and a pair of titties that wouldn't quit.

He adjusted his sunglasses, thinking back to that first night… *Bacardi and Coke…Making out on the backseat of the taxicab.* A semi-regular booty call soon got out of hand, and before he knew it, he was introducing her to his parents.

Seeing a paddleboarder ahead, he smiled, then accelerated at top speed through the turn, kicking up a rooster tail of spray. The poor paddleboarder had seen Chip coming but couldn't get out of the way in time. His eyes opened wide and he quacked—like the sitting duck he was—as Chip sent him head over heels into the drink.

Chip looked back and laughed as he sped away. The floundering paddleboarder swore and shook his fist.

It's good to blow off steam. Fuck Dani.

He stood and pulled back on the throttle, shouting "Yahoo!" as he exited the bay. He could barely hear himself over the thrum of the engine and the splashing of seawater. White beads of spray sparkled and bounced across the surface of the water, dissolving with a hiss.

He trailed a boat for a while, getting air off the back of their wake, before passing the marina, first one buoy, then another, until he was a quarter mile from the shoreline.

His chest and arms had started to ache. It was a good ache, though. *Like any good workout, if you 'aint sore, you 'aint doing it right,* he often told his clients.

To his right, a pod of dolphins swam in formation across a wide sandbar. He headed in that direction, decelerating, but they darted off before he could get a decent look.

He was cruising along a deep channel with sea grass at the bottom when something shot past going in the other direction.

"Yah, holy—!" he said, eyes wide. *What the fuck was that?* It was big—bigger than a dolphin, and moving fast.

It wasn't like him to get spooked by anything. He glanced around, looking for the closest boat, but there were none. He was alone.

A shape bobbed out of the water about 20 feet in front of him. He pulled down his sunglasses and shielded his eyes with the flat of his hand, but the sun obscured his view. The thing submerged, disappearing as quickly as it appeared.

Curious, he pulled back on the throttle, heading over to where he'd last seen it. "Where are you, you, mother—?" He circled slowly, gazing through the water. He had a hollow feeling in his belly.

Suddenly, he saw a shadow moving swiftly and smoothly—as fast as any fish—along the channel.

"Fuck." It was a sort of grayish-green, and it blended perfectly with the seagrass bottom.

WHAM!—Something rammed into the Jet Ski from underneath, pushing the ski up before pulling it back down again.

"Shi-it!" he yelled, losing balance and falling into the water. His life jacket kept him afloat. The ski's engine shut off as the safety lanyard attached to his life jacket was pulled from the switch. The ski coasted away.

Must've been hit by a shark. He started to swim back to the ski. *No. This can't be happening. I'm in the water with an actual freaking shark.*

Something touched his foot. *Shit!* He swam faster.

Oh, thank god. The ski was within arm's length. As he reached to pull himself up, something grabbed him and pulled him under. Sharp pain lanced through his leg, and cold water poured into his torn wetsuit.

The water turned turbulent, and he saw blood—his own blood. He tried to scream but succeeded only in swallowing water. *This can't be happening. Not me. Not now.*

Then...whatever had him let him go, and he bobbed to the surface.

"HELP!" he cried, in agony, almost blind with the pain. "Help! Please!" But there was no one to listen.

He knew he was losing blood, and shaking.

Must be in shock.

WHAM!—something smashed into him, dragging him under. In his mind, he was screaming. He struggled back to the surface, gasping for air. It came back, again and again, battering his body and churning the water. He was terrified. Stunned. Instinct finally took over, and he lashed out, punching, trying to push it away. It thrashed. He couldn't see much, but he saw enough to know it wasn't a shark. Suddenly, he felt a searing pain in his guts. He opened his mouth and took in a lungful of water. A pair of black eyes stared into his. *Oh god. What is it?* He saw a mouth filled with rows of sharp, needle-like teeth before they tore his flesh.

18

Dani sat at the vanity mirror, searching the lines of her face. Lack of sleep was taking its toll. Searching for her hair dryer, her hand brushed against something, which skittered in the drawer. It was the keepsake, the necklace that Eric had given her. It glimmered in the dim light, beautiful and strange. *Curious.* She turned it over in her hand. *It's heavy...gold maybe...with pearl inlays?* Its shape was similar to a shard of coral, and intricately engraved with a strange and twisted relief. Dani first tried to refuse the gift, but Eric had insisted. If he'd meant to impress her, he had. It was unlike any jewelry she'd ever seen. She returned it to the drawer.

I wonder what Eric's doing now? She started to blow-dry her hair. She thought about how they'd kissed, about him pressed against her, his skin still cool and damp from the rain, his hands exploring, their bodies entwined, moving like a freight train, her hips grinding deeper and deeper.

Putting the hairdryer away, she wondered what it would be like to run away with him. *To get up and leave? He'd asked her to come to the Florida Keys with him. Oh, god, am I a bad person for thinking it?* She had to admit it sounded wonderful.

Picking up her cell, she scrolled till she found Eric's number. Biting her thumbnail, she texted: *Hey, I had a great time the other night.* It was the most natural thing she could think to say. She drew in her breath and clicked send.

What am I doing? I'm behaving like a pheromone-addled high-schooler? I deserve to be happy, though, don't I?

She went to the living room and switched on the TV. An episode of Dr. Phil was playing, a re-run—the one where the twenty-year-old claimed to be rapper Eminem's daughter. In typical fashion, Doctor Phil shook his head and tried not to *sugarcoat things*.

Dani yawned before switching channels to the Home Shopping Network. A Gary-Busey-like TV presenter with impossibly white teeth came on, promoting a range of wearable towels. Dani brightened, grabbed her cell and purse from the side stand, and dialed the number on the screen. There was a recorded message. While she waited, she flicked through the credit cards in her wallet till she found one that wasn't maxed out. "Soft Pink," she said when prompted, and entered her card details. Estimated time of delivery: 3 days.

***

In the garage, Dani turned the keys in the ignition and the Honda spluttered to life. She'd decided to go to the park. *The fresh air will do me good.* Only, it had to be at least ninety degrees out. Chip had taken the SUV and hadn't come home that night. *He's probably sulking and has gone to Miami after all.* She pumped the A/C, clicked the remote, and the garage door rolled back.

The park was only a short drive away. She held her breath as she got out and shielded her eyes from the midday sun. *Why did I think this was a good idea?* The heat was coming off the pavement in waves.

There was the scent of freshly mowed lawn as she stepped onto the curb. She gave a nod to the park-goers interspersed on benches, chatting. She sat under a large tree, the shade a welcome reprieve. Droplets of perspiration had formed on her brow. She found herself, already, missing the Honda's A/C.

A couple passed on her right, holding hands, and Dani's shoulders slumped. Chip had looked at her like that once. She sighed. Life seemed so difficult. How had things gone so wrong? *Chip wasn't selfish when we first met. He's changed.* She regretted not having a support circle. Circumstance had robbed her of her parents.

Dani observed a group of mothers gossiping. Suddenly, she felt self-conscious. One of them ignored her child, with her ear glued to her cell, making deals and answering emails, while her son ran around like a maniac, terrorizing the other children.

Her cell vibrated. A message. Dani felt a thrill of excitement. It was Eric: *Hey, so when can I see you again?* She wanted to see him.

19

Mrs. Werner stood by the oven. The air was fragrant with a blend of cinnamon, nutmeg, and vanilla. She wore the novelty *KISS THE COOK* apron her granddaughter had given her one Christmas.

Toby lay on the floor while the ceiling fan whirred overhead, and the radio played *Dream Lover*, by Bobby Darin, in the background.

She checked the peach cobbler. "There. You see," she said to Toby, putting on an oven mitt.

Bobby Darin crooned.

Toby raised his head, then lay back, unperturbed.

"That's how you know it's ready," she said, taking the dish out of the oven and setting it aside to cool. The crisscross of dough strips, on top, had turned a golden brown.

Removing her oven mitt, she went to the window and looked out. Javier was in the yard trimming hedges. She liked the mustachioed gardener. He had a quiet, sensible way about him and an honest face.

She took a glass of lemonade from the counter and sipped before switching off the radio.

Toby half-heartedly wagged his tail.

Suddenly, she felt faint, and the blood drained from her face. It was back—that all-too-familiar heartburn, along with the pressure on her chest. She took a small vial of pills from her tote bag, unscrewed the lid, and set one of the pills under her tongue to dissolve.

The door opened.

"Work is finished, Missus," Javier said.

Toby sat up.

"Come in, Javier." She put the pills away and took out her purse. She felt breathless and had to steady herself against the counter.

"You okay?" Javier leaned in as if to catch her.

"Fine," she said, feeling the blood returning to her face. "Come in, please."

He closed the door and began to remove his shoes. She motioned for him not to bother.

"Is that enough for today's work?" she asked, handing him cash from her purse.

"Yes, is perfeck," he said, folding the bills into his breast pocket.

"Would you like a drink?"

Javier nodded.

She poured him a glass from a pitcher of lemonade. Javier accepted it and drank eagerly.

"How is Antonio?" she asked.

"Good, thank you, Missus," he said. "He really like his bike right now, but homework? Not so much."

"Boys will be boys." She laughed. "And Rosa? How's she?"

"Si, she is good," Javier said. "Excep she sick right now. She have cold."

"That's no good," she said, tutting. "She'll have to get plenty of bed rest and keep up the liquids, won't she?"

"Si." He nodded, taking another mouthful of lemonade.

"I've baked my world-famous peach cobbler. You'll have to take this home to Rosa."

Javier put his lemonade down. "No, Missus, is too much—"

She waved dismissively. "This will help raise her spirits. You can bring the dish back next time."

"Si, okay, Missus,"

"Call me Helen."

***

Dani glanced at the clock on the wall. It was late. *Where is Chip?* He wasn't answering his phone or replying to any of her text messages. She knew he was upset, but he would've replied by now, even if he were still huffy. She'd called all the usual bonehead friends, and they didn't know his whereabouts either. She was worried. In the morning, she would file a missing person report at the police station.

20

It happens again—just as it did before. You're breathing heavily. Your heart is pounding. Adrenaline is pumping. Your gun is drawn. You're back in the Ramírez house. You know you're dreaming. All the colors are extra brilliant and bright, but you dream on anyway. You get to the door.

"Police. Open up!" you say.

No answer.

You've already radioed for backup, but you can't wait. There's somewhere you've got to be. You kick in the door and move rapidly down the hall, senses heightened. There's a trail of blood.

"Police!" you say again. "Come out where I can see you."

You're moving quicker now, up the stairs to the final room. There's that coppery smell, like coins. It's the girl's blood. There's the yellow dress. Blood everywhere. Her stomach has spilled on the floor. You start to hyperventilate. BANG! There's an explosion of pain in your leg. You realize you've been shot.

Officer down! you think, but backup is minutes away. Whirling round, you see Ramírez bearing down on you with a gun.

"Fuck you, copper!" he screams at the top of his lungs, firing wildly. The guy's eyes are fully dilated, his teeth rotten. He's out of his gourd on methamphetamine.

You aim. If you hesitate, you're good as dead. You squeeze the trigger. BANG!

Frank woke to the sound of ringing. He fumbled for the phone on the night-stand. "Hello?" Perspiration clung to his face, back, and arms.

"Sergeant Hagen?" the voice on the other end asked.

He coughed. "Who's this?"

"Andy Benson. From forensics."

"Oh hey, Andy," he said, sitting up. "Do you know what time it is?"

"Sorry for calling so early, but I think you'd better come to Central Beach."

"Why? What's the problem?"

"We've got a floater down here."

"A drowning?"

"Not exactly. You'd better come see."

Around thirty minutes later, Frank arrived at Central Beach. He glimpsed the white sand beach, in between buildings, as soon as he pulled up along the Boulevard. The sky was overcast, an onshore breeze whipping the lines of palm trees by the road.

He walked down the beach with his hands in his pockets, turning his face from the wind-kicked sand, which stung his cheeks. A cargo ship was visible on the horizon behind a low-hanging haze. The emotional aftermath from the dream still lingered. He felt tired and an odd sense of foreboding.

His leg ached. The sand was difficult to walk on, despite it being dry and compacted. The hunt for Proteus was not going well. They'd had some replies to their fake profiles on *D8Swift*, sure, but none of the would-be-suitors fit the bill. Not really. *Bunch of college kids and divorcees.*

He scanned the beach, a sprawling expanse of sand, littered with the occasional cigarette butt and bottle cap. He passed an unmanned lifeguard tower, and a mound of seaweed, by the shoreline. The forensics team was already there.

"Frank!" said Andy, wearing his forensic suit. "Thanks for coming. This way. Some joggers found it."

Frank rolled his eyes. "Why is it always the joggers who find this shit?" He followed him, then stopped. Driftwood and weeds were clumped together in the shape of a body.

Andy leaned down and pulled back the seaweed to reveal a mottled gray face. "Must've washed ashore last night."

Frank saw tattered flesh and exposed bone. Bile rose in his throat. Pieces of the face were missing. "Something's made a meal of it?"

Andy nodded. He pointed to the corpse's arms. "Missing Persons are looking for a Chip Kuwolski—a personal trainer from Dorland Park—with these same tattoos. The wife said he went Jet Skiing a few days ago. Never came home.

"I was thinking…shark attack…but Creepy, at the ME's office, said to give you a call. Said it might be linked to some homicides?"

"Creepy said that?" Frank furrowed his brow, crouched, and used a piece of driftwood to lift the weeds away.

"You looking for something in particular?" Andy asked.

"Maybe," Frank said, but then he saw it: a tiny puncture wound an inch below the sternum.

21

Melissa Harris, 23, stood in the bathroom of the Blue Jay nightclub, over by a set of sinks. She had blonde, shoulder-length hair, and wore a figure-hugging yellow dress. She was on a date and was nervous.

Like you? C'mon, why wouldn't he like you? fixing her makeup in the mirror. *There…I'd date you.*

The bathroom door burst open and the sounds of the club filtered in. Melissa busied herself with her makeup as several inebriated girls, laughing and chatting, entered, and made their way to the stalls against the wall.

Melissa hiccupped and flattened the wrinkles on her dress, sucking in her breath. She felt a little inebriated herself. *Too many cosmos.* She'd broken the seal now, which meant a trip to the bathroom in regular five-minute intervals. *Curse this tiny bladder.* On the wall was an ad touting the merits of drinking responsibly.

She washed her hands with liquid soap and examined the necklace her date had given her, in the mirror. It glimmered under the down lights, with each subtle rise and fall of her breast. It was heavy, gold, and covered with intricate pearl inlays. She had tried to refuse the gift, but he wouldn't hear of it.

She shook her hands in the sink. *Who gives a gift like this on a first date anyway? He must be a kook.* She took a paper towel from the dispenser, drying her hands. *But he's a kook with money. Who would've thought dealing in art would have been so lucrative? He must be rolling in it like Bigshot Moneybags if he can afford this.*

The girls exited the stalls, their chatter obnoxiously loud. One of the girls flashed a smile at Melissa before washing their hands. They left the bathroom, the electric hand dryer still blasting.

Jack Gilman. What kind of name is Gilman? Irish maybe? She shrugged. "Melissa Gilman," she said, aloud, trying how it sounded. *Getting ahead of ourselves, aren't we?*

She had met Jack using an online dating app called *D8Swift. Find your Type with just one swipe,* proclaimed the apps tagline—which appealed to her, because she was normally shy and found it difficult to meet people. She was looking for more than a casual hookup; she was looking for a significant other. It wasn't the first dating app she'd used, and had been on a couple of dates before. Neither was boyfriend material. One was a technician at a local cell phone repair store, while the other was an inventor—which was code for, *'I live in my grandma's basement.'* Jack was different, though. He was the first date she felt genuinely attracted to. She'd taken one look at his profile, at that jawline and chiseled cheekbones, and thought, *'Hello! Now I know what I want for my birthday.' Honestly, it should be illegal to be that good-looking.*

Now she'd met him, in person, she found him even

more irresistible. He was charming, had dark, alluring eyes, and exuded an air of confidence.

He said he's thirty-five—admittedly, that's quite an age gap. The age thing never bothered Jay-Z and Beyoncé, though. It never bothered Mary-Kate Olsen and that banker guy.

She checked her reflection in the mirror again—the necklace glimmered and glowed—before exiting the bathroom.

22

"Are you still having the dreams?" Buchinsky asked.

"Uh-huh," Dani said.

"Interesting. What about the associated feeling of dread?"

Dani shrugged. "It hasn't gone away."

Buchinsky frowned. "Is the Prozac helping, though?"

"I've stopped crying, if that means anything?"

"Good, it should help with the anxiety."

Dani sighed, rubbing her neck. "I think I misplaced my scarf the last time I was here. You haven't seen it, have you?"

He shook his head. "We'll give the medication a while longer before varying the dose, okay?"

She crossed her legs.

"How are things with you and Chip?"

"Okay, I guess," she said, looking at her feet. "I mean, we've been better."

Buchinsky brightened. "Remember, there are no perfect marriages, just imperfect people."

Dani slumped her shoulders. "I guess Chip and I are more imperfect than most."

"What's the problem?" Buchinsky tilted his head.

She snorted. "It's Chip, so...where do I start?"

"Would you care to expand on that?"

"Chip promises to do things, then doesn't follow through. He's impulsive. Irresponsible. Plus, there's the gambling."

Buchinsky cleared his throat. "Did you talk with him about my suggestion? Will he come to one of our sessions?"

Dani rolled her eyes. "I spoke with him. He won't come. He doesn't believe in therapy."

Buchinksy gave a condescending smile. "That's okay. Some individuals fear the change therapy can instigate in their lives. You should keep trying, though."

Danni nodded. "We don't see eye to eye on a lot of things. We argue a lot—he has a bad temper. I'll ask him to do something, and he flakes. He thinks a woman's place is in the home, so it's my job to do everything."

"Go on," Buchinsky said. "I'd like to hear about that."

"Do you know what he did?" Dani said, indignantly. "He bought a Jet Ski using our joint savings, after I specifically told him not to."

"Really?" Buchinsky said.

"We had a terrible fight, and, now, he's run off—probably to Miami, with some of his buddies."

"Do you know that for sure?"

She shrugged. "He's done it before. He's never been what you might call reliable. He's taken our other car, and that Jet Ski. He's self-centred. So, no, things aren't great between us."

Buchinsky scribbled another note. "Will you patch

things up, do you think?"

There was a long pause.

She held a fist to her lips. "I've been trying to decide whether or not to tell you. I was hoping I wouldn't chicken out."

"I want you to feel like you can share in here, Dani," he said, sitting forward. He removed his glasses, and put a hand on hers. "This is a safe space."

"I've started seeing someone," she said, pulling her hand away.

Buchinsky swallowed. "Someone who's not Chip?"

Dani nodded. "Eric."

Buchinsky sat back in his chair. "I'm not here to judge, but having an affair can add a lot of unneeded stress and baggage to a marriage."

She sighed. "Things between Chip and I haven't been good for a while. I realize I've been treading water, trying to think of a way to end it."

Buchinsky grimaced. "I understand. It can be painful realizing your marriage is over."

Dani nodded. "I like, Eric. I've never been this in love with anyone. I think about him all the time."

He coughed. "Can you see yourself in a lasting relationship with…Eric?"

Dani considered this. "I like him. He's nice to me."

"Maybe you should tell Chip how you feel. It pays to be open about these things."

"You're right. I'll tell him—as soon as he turns up."

23

Frank raised his hand, hesitated, then knocked on the door. A moment passed, he heard footsteps and the door opened. A woman in her thirties, with brown hair, fair skin, and freckles, answered.

"Mrs. Kowalski?" Frank asked. It was a hot day and he was happy to be in the shade. His old leg wound ached—it always did when a change of weather was coming.

"Arr, no. I'm her friend, Beth." She tilted her head. "And you are?"

He scanned either side. It was a nice street, peaceful. He regretted he would be the bearer of bad news. "Detective Hagen, ma'am. I'm with the FLPD. Is Mrs. Kowalski home? It's important I speak with her."

Beth frowned. "Wait here."

She disappeared inside.

Frank hated this part of the job. Whenever possible, he sent a uniformed officer to notify next of kin that a loved one had died. It was *unusual* for the investigating officer to do such a task, but he made an exception in this instance. He wanted to be there if there was even the slightest chance he could shed light on the case.

Beth returned a short while later, with another woman in tow. She had mousy blonde hair, pale, light blue eyes, and wore an artist's apron.

"Mrs. Kowalski?" Frank asked.

She opened her mouth to speak, then paused. "You better come in."

***

"I can't believe it," Dani said, crying. "I can't believe he's dead."

They were sitting around the kitchen table. Frank had already broken the news of Chip's violent death, suspected murder, and the ongoing investigation. He gave her his handkerchief.

"Thank you," she said, using it to dry her tears.

Beth rubbed her friend's back in a comforting gesture. "Are you sure it's him?"

Frank nodded. "His tattoos matched the photos Dani gave police. We found his car, abandoned, at Colohatchee boat ramp."

"Shit." Beth's shoulders slumped.

Dani buried her face in her hands.

"Of course, we will still need you, Dani, to come to the Medical Examiner's Office, to formally identify the body."

She nodded.

"Are there any other family members to notify?" Frank asked.

"There's Chip's dad in Jacksonville," Dani said. "And his sister in Gainesville."

"We're going to need their addresses."

Dani rose and located them in a little book she kept in a drawer.

Frank jotted these down. "We'll, also, need you to pick up Chip's personal items. There's the SUV, of course, and wedding ring."

Dani nodded.

"I have some questions to ask as part of the investigation. Is that okay?"

"Okay," Dani said.

Beth chewed on a fingernail.

"Thank you," Frank said, taking her hand and squeezing it.

"Do you know if Chip had any enemies?"

Dani raised her eyebrows. "Who Chip? No, not really. I mean, he could be difficult sometimes—he had a short fuse—but he made friends easily."

Frank nodded, and noted this in his notepad. "Do you remember him arguing with anyone? Or, perhaps, he owed someone money?"

Dani shrugged.

"Not really. I mean, the last time I saw him we'd argued, but that was because he'd bought that stupid Jet Ski. I told him not to, but he went and did it anyway. When he didn't come home, I assumed he was still angry and thought he'd gone to Miami with some buddies.

"Are you going to catch whoever did this, Detective?" Beth interjected.

"We're going to do our best," Frank said. "At this stage, though, we're still not sure if the perp is a who or a *what*. I mean, the circumstances of his death…it would be easy to write it off as a shark attack. But I'm not so sure."

"Are you thinking maybe someone dumped him, and dressed it up to look like a shark attack?" asked Beth.

"Maybe," Frank said. "In any case, we're going to find out what happened." He gave a reassuring smile.

**

Frank was midway down the driveway when he heard a voice.

"Hey, Detective!"

He turned and saw Beth had followed.

She was out of breath.

"Is everything okay?" he asked.

She bit her lip. "Umm, yes. I mean, no. Heck, I don't know what I mean. My friend just lost her husband, so there's that...I just wanted to say thank you, y'know? For the kindness you showed back there."

"Don't mention it."

"No, really, you're a stand-up guy—I can see that. God knows there's a deficit of those in the world right now. Are you going to find out what happened to Chip?"

"We'll do our damndest." Frank looked towards the house. "She's pretty upset right now, but it will pass. If you think of anything else that might be pertinent to the case, let me know." He handed her his card.

24

Dani stepped onto the rear porch, the screen door swinging shut behind her. There was a lump in her throat and she felt short of breath. *I can't believe he's dead.* Chip had been hurtful and self-centred, but she still loved him. They were friends, lovers, confidants. *Oh god, I feel so abandoned.* There came the distant rumble of thunder.

Dani had sensed the change coming; there was the telltale drop in temperature; the very air resonating with the energy of the encroaching storm. She wrung her hands and sobbed. *It just hurts so much. Why was he taken so soon?*

The porch was fully enclosed by insect screens, as the mosquitoes were innumerable at that time of year. Dani paced back and forth, then stopped, looking into the inky darkness of the night. What little breeze there had been was replaced with an eerie calm. The yard, patchy and weed ridden, terminated with an ivy-covered wire fence and the waterway. A flash of lightning illuminated everything; the water's surface, a mass of quicksilver.

Dani exhaled heavily. The police had given the

SUV back that morning, along with Chip's wedding ring. The autopsy report had given all the grisly details. *Poor Chip.* It was unthinkable—the sheer brutality. *Trust him to depart this life with a mystery.*

Dani blinked back tears. She was in shock. Chip's death had been sudden and caught her off guard. After several years of marriage, she realized she would never speak to him again. *What I would give to speak to him...* A vein of white lightning lit the black marble sky, and again she heard the deep boom of thunder. *That storm is getting close.*

She dabbed at her face with her palm. *I feel empty, like...there's a black hole where my heart used to be.* Lightning flashed again, and a hundred fire-flags danced to the tune of thunder. *Maybe he was called home—by a higher power.*

Tears streamed down Dani's cheeks, as she thought of happier moments with Chip. *How could this happen? Where's the justice?*

There has to be something else to feel happy about. She slid her hand into her pocket and found her cell phone. *Eric! He won't mind.*

She dialed his number. "C'mon...pick up." She gave up after six rings. "Where is he? He's from out of town. It's not like he has a busy social calendar."

From across the water, she heard the echoey sound of a dog barking. *The poor thing.* Its anxious barks became higher-pitched and more insistent. *Where's your owner?*

She sniffed while absent-mindedly scrolling through her phone, till she came to the last text message from Eric: *When can I see you again?* She stared at backlit screen, the blinking cursor staring back, as she rehearsed her reply in her mind. *Tomorrow*, she keyed in and hit send.

Lightning cracked and thunder rumbled as the storm finally broke. The heavens opened and the rain fell in a deluge, drumming out a rhythm on the porch roof. The wind gusted, and it grew cold. Dani went inside.

25

Steam billowed from the shower recess as Helen stepped onto a soaking bath mat. She dried herself vigorously, making sure to rub her aching joints, before wrapping herself in a towel. Years of stooping over a canvas and gripping a paintbrush were paying their toll. A hot shower of an evening helped with her circulation. In the bedroom, she dried her hair and put it in curlers, swapping her towel for a nightie.

Law & Order played on the television in the living room. She sat in the recliner. The TV show's iconic intro was gratifying to her ears. She liked everything about the police procedural, including Sam Waterston.

Switching on the lamp, she realized the doggie bed in the corner was empty.

"Toby?"

Nothing.

Feeling a chill, she got up and put on her slippers and dressing gown. A change was coming.

Walking down the hall, past the framed photos of family and friends, to the kitchen, she heard the deep boom of thunder, followed by the sound of barking. *Toby's outside*. There was the glimmer of lightning, and his barks became an anxious yapping.

"Gosh. What in the Sam Hill has gotten into you, Toby?" She turned on the patio light and stepped outside.

The yard ended in a ledge overlooking the waterway. It took a while for her eyes to adjust. Toby paced back and forth along the ledge, barking furiously. His doggy barks echoed across the water. Meanwhile, streaks of lightning rent the sky.

"Toby. Come here, Toby!"

He stopped barking and ran to her, his collar making a bell-like tinkle. "I don't understand it. You're usually petrified of storms." She gave the little dog a pat and went inside.

***

Helen awoke to the sound of the drumming rain. The room was stuffy. *It's late.* She rolled onto her side, shifting the covers. The red glowing numbers on her digital alarm clock read 1:11 AM. *No, maybe it's early.* She turned back over. *My feet are cold. Where's Toby?* The part of the bed where the terrier usually curled was bare.

She became aware of a far-away, insistent barking. *Am I imagining this?* She tried to pinpoint the direction. It dawned on her—Toby was outside yapping in the rain.

The—*tick, tack*—of the rain sounded against the window as she threw off the covers and forced herself out of bed. *The silly dog is out there getting wet. I'll have to soil a towel to dry the little scoundrel.*

For the second time that evening—putting on her

slippers and gown—she walked down the hall to the kitchen, switched on the patio light, and stepped outside. The first raindrops touched her skin, wet and cold. She tried to make herself as narrow as possible, staying under the eaves.

The little terrier—she saw through the inky blackness—was pacing by the water's edge, barking furiously.

"Toby. Toby. Come," she said, trying to keep her voice low, being mindful of the neighbors.

Thunder crashed.

"Hush, Toby," she hissed. But he kept on barking.

"Ooo, you little…" She went inside to fetch Toby's leash, as well as a raincoat, which she slipped on over her nightgown.

"I can't believe you," she said, coming back outside. *The little stinker is actually going to make me go and get him.* She stepped from under the eaves, putting up the hood of her raincoat.

"Toby," she hissed again, walking down the path.

The little terrier continued to bark furiously.

She tried to tiptoe around the muddy puddles.

Toby had whipped himself into a barking frenzy, pacing along the ledge at the end of the yard, bopping up and down on his forepaws like the cartoon dog from *Tom and Jerry*.

"What's gotten into you?" she said again, stooping to clip the leash on the little dog's collar. Toby dodged the first couple of attempts. She managed it on the third try, picking him up.

"What's the matter?" she said. Toby wriggled and squirmed, and she struggled to keep hold.

"Honestly, Toby. What do you think—"

She wiped the rain from her face. Something was wrong. She felt it in the pit of her stomach. It made her skin crawl. The air was charged somehow.

Toby went right on barking, his lip curled back, fangs bared. All his attention appeared to be on the water.

Lightning flashed.

Helen stopped. Her eyes were drawn to a spot about thirty feet out on the water, to a set of ever-widening ripples.

Thunder roared and there was another flash of lightning.

Helen gasped, taking a step back, making a sound halfway between a moan and a whimper. Something was there in the dark. It had disturbed the surface of the water. She had seen its shape, its outline, although she couldn't make it out clearly. It had disappeared as quickly as it had appeared. Its sinuous movement reminded her of the cresting backbone of a dolphin or shark. Both came up into the waterways from time to time, she'd heard. *Perhaps it's a gator? No, no, that isn't it.* This was something else. Suddenly she felt very exposed standing there by herself, in the rain.

"C'mon, let's go," she said, to the still barking terrier, starting her way back to the house.

The rain came down in sheets.

She felt uneasy walking back, and couldn't shake the feeling of being watched. It gave her gooseflesh. Helen tightened the hood of her raincoat. Her slippers were sopping wet, caked in mud, and each footfall made a vacuum-like squelch as she pulled free.

She thought she heard the sound of heavy footsteps behind her, out of time with her own. She reassured herself it was just her imagination. *Nope. Uh-uh. I don't like this.* Panting with exertion, she quickened her pace.

In her haste, she slipped and lost her footing, letting go of Toby, and landed face first in the mud. A twinge of pain shot up her wrist.

Toby, who'd landed on his feet, had his hackles up and was still barking.

"Dammit all," she said. With no small amount of effort, she pushed herself up until she was kneeling, and flexed her wrist—near as she could tell, it wasn't broken. Mud was on her face and in her hair. Her dressing gown was soaked and she had lost her slippers. Taking Toby's leash in hand, she stood, making a futile effort to wipe away the mud.

She sensed she was being watched. Looking behind her, she saw something that made her freeze. Her mouth fell open. A vague hulking figure, more like a shadow than a person, stood twenty feet away, watching.

She shrieked and ran barefoot the rest of the way, pulling Toby along by the leash; the back-patio light shone like a lighthouse beacon in the dark. She and Toby ran up the stairs and into the house, shutting the door behind them.

Dear god! She pressed her back to the door. Her heart raced, pounding like a drum. The tightness in her chest was acute, and she felt dizzy. *The light!* She whirled around, switching off the back-patio light.

Did I imagine that? She paused and took a deep breath. *It's late. The mind can play funny tricks.*

She peered through the frosted glass panels of the door but saw nothing. Her eyes needed to adjust. Then, a flash of lightning illuminated a tall shape blocking the doorway.

She screamed, dropping Toby's leash and backing away. *Whatever you are, stay the fuck away.* Her eyes widened, suddenly remembering she leaped and bolted the door.

Toby barked furiously.

She pressed a muddy fist to her mouth to stifle a scream. Her eyes went to the wall-mounted telephone.

The door handle turned then stopped, as if being tested by the nameless intruder.

Toby barked.

Thunder boomed.

Helen shook her head. *This can't be happening. If only Earl were here, he'd know what to do. Or, if Aaron weren't a million miles away...*

"But they're not." Suddenly she felt short of breath.

The door rattled in its frame, and she took another step back. *Whatever it is...it wants in.*

The glass panels fell to the floor and shattered.

Toby barked in outrage.

Rousing herself from her malaise, she ran to the phone and began dialing 911. But, as she dialed, Toby bolted through the flap of the doggie door.

Dropping the phone, a mortified Helen dove for Toby's leash, seizing the end, wrapping it around her wrist before it disappeared. She felt the terrier pulling, until she heard a god-awful yelp, followed by a deafening silence. The leash went slack.

"No!" she cried.

Without warning, she was hauled—by the leash, still in her hand—screaming and sliding across the linoleum, until she collided with the solid, wooden door, stopping with a sickening thud.

Her head throbbed and her vision was a kaleidoscope of pins and needles. She put a hand up, feeling the heat of blood pouring from her crown. The vicelike pressure in her chest was back, along with the sensation of an arrhythmic heartbeat.

She tried to rise then slumped. The tote bag with her pills was on the table, out of reach. Her breathing became labored, and she felt a stabbing pain in her chest and arms.

She wheezed something unintelligible, while reaching for the phone. It was futile. *Beep, Beep, Beep—* went the handset.

26

Unceremoniously sprawled on the kitchen floor lay the body of an elderly woman. She rested in a pool of drying blood with shards of broken glass scattered about her.

Forensics were already at the scene, bagging evidence and dusting for prints.

Frank took in the details of the room: the ancient oven, the tacky linoleum floor, the macramé on the wall; the décor was dated, but it was clean.

He took his notepad from his pocket. *Who would do this to a lonely, old lady?* The intermittent flashing of the crime scene photographer's camera interrupted his train of thought.

Frank knelt beside the body. The victim wore a raincoat over her dressing gown and nightie, and her hair—done up in curlers—was matted with dry blood. *Roughly 24 hours is my guess.* He jotted this down.

Frank, noticing the handset of the wall-mounted telephone, still hanging from its spiral cord, thought, *Who'd you try to call?* His eyes narrowed.

He checked his notes…

HELEN WERNER. NOTED ARTIST.
SPOUSE? NONE/ WIDOW.
OTHER FAMILY?
RAINCOAT? HEAD INJURY?

He harrumphed. *Better check the records with the phone company later.*

Frank rubbed his five o'clock shadow. The door was still bolted from the inside, the only signs of forced entry: the smashed glass. *It's not burglary.* The wedding band was still attached to Werner's finger, and there were other valuables around the room.

He observed her raincoat and muddy, bare feet. *Okay, so you went outside—but why?* There was a trail of mud across the linoleum from the center of the room to the body. *Jesus. You were dragged?*

Something on the breakfast nook caught his attention: a tote bag. He stuck his hand in and fished out a vial of pills. NITRO-GLYC-ERIN, the label read. He frowned and returned the pills to where he found them.

Scared? Possible heart attack?

Seeing the doggy flap in the door, Frank turned to one of the forensic guys and asked, "Did she have a dog?"

The forensic guy nodded. "Maltese terrier. The gardener found it, out back, with its neck broken."

Frank winced. "Gardener?"

The forensic guy pointed to a mustachioed man standing with some uniformed cops in the hall.

***

"And that's when you called 911?" Frank asked.

"Si," Javier said. "First, I knock on front door, but no one answer, so I go 'round back. That's when I see broken glass."

Javier was short but solidly built—evidence of a working life spent outdoors. He looked down and sniffed.

"You came to work on the garden?" Frank asked.

"Was returning dish," Javier said, pointing to an oven dish on the counter.

Frank nodded. "So, I take it you and Werner were close?"

Javier shrugged. "I work here for years."

"I see," Frank said, scribbling a note in his notebook.

Javier cleared his throat. "Mrs. Werner—I mean Helen—she was a nice woman. Who would do this?"

"I don't know, Mister Diaz, but we're going to find out."

Javier shook his head. "They even *keel* dog."

***

Outside, the ground was sodden and muddy from the storm. It was a medium-sized yard with several low-cut trees and rows of freshly trimmed hedges down either side. Frank stopped at a ledge at the foot of the garden, overlooking the water. Standing there and surveying the glassy surface of the bay made him feel uneasy. He shifted his weight. Something about the case didn't feel right.

Frank picked up a stone and flung it so it skipped across the surface of the water. He cleared his throat then took a step back from the ledge. He was ordering and reordering things in his mind. Moments before they found the old lady's slippers, outside, caked in mud. *What would have scared her so bad she would have left them in the rain?*

What struck Frank, too, was the brutality of the attacker. *Or, is it attackers? There could have been more than one assailant.* He sighed. *This wasn't your typical break-in and enter. Heck, a blind man could tell that.*

He knelt next to where they found the dog. It still wore its leash. The collar had a name tag, which he turned over in his hand. "Toby, huh? Well, sorry pal. You deserved better than this. What can you tell me, hey?"

Looking the dog over, Frank noticed something lodged in its mouth. He took his pen and pried the animal's teeth apart. After scraping the object into a plastic evidence bag, he held it up to examine it. It appeared to be a piece of leathery skin. Frank frowned, made sure no one was watching, then slipped it into his pocket.

27

Dani awoke on the berth of the main cabin. She sat up and yawned, tussling her hair. Light poured in through the starboard porthole. It took her a moment to realize she was still aboard Eric's boat. The air still lingered with the scent of his cologne. She smiled, her cheeks flush with the memory of the night they'd shared.

She rose from bed and stretched, sensing the rocking of the boat. *How did I get off the dock?* It didn't make sense. Normally, she would have been so afraid. *Eric must have helped.*

Padding down the passageway to the main living area, she found him in the galley making a pot of coffee.

"Morning, sleepy head," he said, as she sat on the lounge.

Light shone through the butterfly hatch in the ceiling. He leaned in and kissed her, closing his laptop on the fold-out table, before handing her a cup of coffee. "So, last night was fun."

"It was," she said, accepting the cup. "I can't stop smiling. I love being close to you. Feeling...connected."

He smiled.

She sipped her coffee, using the cup to warm her hands. *Things are different now—more relaxed. As callous as it might sound, now that Chip is gone, there's nothing to feel guilty about.* She was free to love Eric without judgment, unburdened, unfettered. They were just two lonely people finding pleasure in each other's company. "Can I ask you something?"

"Of course." He sat down.

"What are we doing?"

He looked at her quizzically.

"I mean…what are we to each other? Is this just sex or is this something…real?"

He set his coffee aside. "Oh, this is real. I'm right here with you, Dani. You know that? I'm all in."

She grinned. "Oh, good. Because I like you, too."

He put his hand on hers.

"I'm going through something—in case you couldn't tell. Chip's passing among other things." She swept a lock of hair behind her ear. "I just wanted you to know you're helping. I appreciate you."

"You're welcome," he said, and they kissed.

The sound of Dani's cell phone chirping interrupted the silence.

"That's weird," she said, rising to answer it.

"Dani darling. It's Jane," said the voice on the other end. The normally energetic woman sounded more subdued than usual.

"Hi, Jane. This is unexpected. How can I—"

"I have bad news."

"Oh, is everything alright?"

"Helen Werner's died."

"What? Oh no, that's terrible," Dani said, putting

a hand over her mouth. "What happened?"

"It's hard to explain on the phone," Jane said. "The police aren't giving much information, but it looks like she was murdered—can you believe it?"

Dani was taken aback. She didn't like the woman, but no one deserved that. *First Chip. Now Helen Werner?* It felt surreal, like she'd stepped onto the pages of some schlocky horror novel.

"Hello, Dani? Are you still there?"

"Huh? Sorry. I needed a moment to process."

"That's understandable," Jane said. "I did, too, when I first heard the news. We're all in a shock here at the gallery. Anyways...this isn't the only reason for my call. With Helen having passed, this now opens that exhibition slot again. It's yours if you want it? I wish it were under brighter circumstances, but there it is."

"Oh, Jane? I'm not sure what to say."

Jane chuckled. "You could say, yes, darling."

"Well...yes, then."

"Good," Jane said. "I'll have Olivia email you the agreement."

When the call ended, Dani turned to Eric and said. "You're not going to believe it," and she recounted the conversation.

"That's great news," Eric said. "I guess congratulations are in order."

Dani was taken aback. "Didn't you hear what I said? Someone died."

Eric smiled. "You didn't like the woman. Couldn't have happened to a better person. Anyway, you should be happy...you got what you wanted. You got the exhibition slot."

"She didn't deserve to be murdered, though. I

never would have wished that on her."

Eric shrugged. "You're too good a person, Dani. I'm not saying you did. It's all taken care of now, though, isn't it? It's all worked out."

Dani shook her head, disbelieving. *How can he be so heartless?* Something didn't add up. She couldn't reconcile the difference between the warm, sensitive man she thought she knew with the flippant, cold-hearted way he just reacted.

"Do you mind if I grab a shower?" she said. "I need to get ready for work."

Eric nodded. "You can use the head in the main cabin."

Dani looked in a bathroom drawer, while the shower was running, and her breath caught, for inside were half-a-dozen gold necklaces with pearl inlays, just like the one Eric had given her. *Why does he have these? Is he using these to bed naïve women—to buy their love?* She shut the shower off and got dressed.

Eric was on his laptop in the main living area.

"What's this?" she said, throwing a fistful of jewelry on the table. "Why do you have these? You made a show of giving me that necklace? I thought it was one of a kind. I thought I was special?"

"Dani, please calm down. I can explain?"

"Are these for your other girlfriends? Am I just another lay?"

"What? No. They're from a client. When you travel as much as I do, it pays not to have everything in cash. Sometimes—"

She raised her palm. "I think I'd better go."

"Dani?" Eric called after her.

28

Dani stood in her studio, painting another of her seascapes, while David Bowie's *Slow Burn* played in her earphones. She took a Prozac pill and washed it down with wine.

Not the best idea, but what the hell.

Using a flat brush, she blocked in the sky, and the beach in the foreground. The music helped to soothe her aching heart. *Why did Eric have all that jewelry?* The necklaces matched the one he'd given her. It had been a symbol of his commitment. *Did that mean nothing?*

"Oh, god, how could I have trusted him?" Hot tears ran down her face. She painted in the surging waves, their crests, the breakers, and the foam. *Should I go back to him? Were we even exclusive?* softening the edges in the painting, her brushstrokes, moving faster and faster, darting across the canvas with ease.

Soon everything dissolved, and she experienced the expansion, the trance-like state. She had fallen through the canvas into the private world, the middle-place where memory, dream, and reality overlapped. The painting was so life-like, she fancied she could hear the rolling of the waves.

She painted in a boat. It was so detailed its sails billowed in the night breeze. It was getting closer…closer.

Dani gasped and removed her earphones, breaking herself from the trance. *What was that?* It was a presence she'd felt before—from a long ago. She couldn't place it. She set her brush aside, stood back from the easel, and sighed.

Her phone beeped. It was a message from Eric. He wanted her back—to salvage things. Dani began to text, then stopped, turning her phone to silent.

29

"Mom wasn't the nurturing type." The portly, middle-aged man, in Buchinsky's office, sniffed and shifted in his chair. "She never hugged me."

Buchinsky scribbled in his notebook. It was the last appointment of the day. Patients frequently sought this timeslot thinking it would offer more individualized attention. This was fine by Buchinsky; he simply charged a higher fee. He offered the man a Kleenex. "You have the right to feel sad, Jeffrey. The relationship one forms with their mother is significant, formative. Do you think she has trouble expressing her love? Some people struggle to exhibit nurturing behaviours."

The man dabbed at his tears. "She's incapable of love. I hate her." His eyes widened. "Oh, jeez. Did I say that out loud? That's terrible, isn't it?"

"It's okay to feel angry," Buchinsky said, summoning what little empathy he had left. "Most people would feel the same in your situation. Acknowledging your feelings is an important step to healing. Let's explore that."

Jeffrey nodded, looking at the Persian rug. "She was always overbearing, overly critical...a perfectionist." He fidgeted. "She drove Dad away with her constant badgering. Does this mean I had a bad mom? I don't know." He blew his nose. "She kept a roof over our heads, I guess. But at the same time, she would call me fat and stupid—because of my school grades. I didn't find out till later I had dyslexia."

Buchinsky subtly glanced at his watch. He wanted to wrap up soon. "It sounds like you've been carrying a lot on your shoulders."

Jeffrey nodded. "I saw her at my sister's wedding recently. She commented on my clothes. I had to say, '*You know what, Mom, yes, I have gained a little weight. So, what?*'"

"That's awful," Buchinsky said. He coughed then glanced again at his watch. "Shoot—that's the timer. Can we pick up from here next session?"

Jeffrey dabbed at more tears, rose, and shook hands with the doctor.

"In the meantime," Buchinsky said, removing his eyeglasses, "I would offer this feedback. It's important to be kind to yourself. Don't let the relationship you had with your mother shape your other relationships. I'm here for you. There are strategies we can work on together next session, okay?"

Buchinsky waited till Jeffrey shuffled from the room before locking the door. *'Be kind to yourself?'* He felt a twinge of self-loathing. The man had bared his soul, and he offered him empty platitudes. He shook his head.

After a quick once-around returning books to shelves, fanning the magazines on the sideboard, and straightening furniture, he took the box of Kleenex and deposited himself in his desk chair. His wife, Eleanor, wouldn't expect him home till later as he needed to work back late—which was true, in a manner of speaking.

He opened his desk drawer, and inside was a piece of light blue fabric. It was Dani Kowalski's scarf. Originally he'd kept it to give back to her, but then... Buchinsky eyed it for a moment before picking it up. It felt smooth and luxurious to touch. Dani was an attractive woman—so much more than his *other* lady patients. He felt compelled to fix her, to rescue her. He got off on it. Burying his nose in the scarf, he inhaled deeply. It smelled like *her*: floral, sweet, and pungent. He unzipped his pants and began to masturbate, the tip of his penis barely visible from below his extended belly, the flying toasters on his laptop screensaver cascading. The sounds of the traffic, below, drifted through the open window. He fantasized about her, about Dani...

They were in one of their sessions. She was demure, vulnerable, and attentive. *"We shouldn't,"* he would say, all suave and worldly. *"It will get in the way of our professional relationship. We need to be respectful of boundaries."* But she would put a hand on his knee and look at him with soft eyes. They'd kiss deeply and passionately. He'd thrill at the sensation of their locked lips, their tongues gliding. Then she'd sink down and pleasure him with her fervent mouth.

He gave a guttural moan, his stroking motions growing more vigorous. All the while he dreamed of what their life would be like together.

Would she run away with me?

He came with the force of a thunderbolt. The post-orgasm warmth left him temporarily weakened. Then came the detached feelings of worthlessness and guilt. He put the scarf back in a drawer for safekeeping.

Afterwards, he packed his satchel-bag and locked the office. His Mercedes was in the downstairs garage. He started the car and ascended the levels, exiting the car park. The sun had already set, and the city lights had come on. The Mercedes travelled slowly—stop-start, stop-start—through traffic-clogged street. He was on his way home but first…a detour.

***

Dani lived in a quaint, little house, on a tree-lined street in Dorland Park. Buchinsky had learned to recognize it from the tall palm tree in the front yard. He pulled up to the curb, opposite, and shut off his headlights. The house was in silhouette except for the orange glow from one of the downstairs windows.

He opened the centre console, took out a set of night vision binoculars and scanned the house. His mouth was dry. He increased the magnification as a shadow flit past the illuminated window. *Dani?* His pulse quickened.

He longed to knock on the door and profess his love to her. He'd tell her he was concerned for her— *which is only natural, seeing I'm her therapist, right?* She'd have to invite him in, because…that was the thing to do. *'Come in,'* she'd say, and she'd offer him a drink. Then *this* would lead to *that*, and before long they'd move to the bedroom.

He glanced at his reflection in the rear-view mirror. *I'm not a pervert. We would be happy together. She will make me happy.*

He took a deep breath, undid his safety belt, and opened the driver's side door. He was halfway across the street when the light in the downstairs window went out. *Shit!* He froze, his heartbeat racing. He'd lost his nerve. Beating a hasty retreat, he got back in the car and drove off.

30

The exhibition room at Vanguard Galleries smelled of wood polish. Patrons, customers, and other artists milled around while soft music played in the background. They spoke in low voices, wandering from room to room, admiring the framed paintings on the wall.

Dani chewed her thumbnail. *Relax. I have to relax.* After refining her art skills for so long, she was experiencing her first solo exhibition. Unbelievable. She was a bona fide artist now. No one could refute that. It *was* an important step.

Jane Brennan, the gallery owner, sashayed towards her.

"Dani da-arling, how are you holding up?"

Dani gulped. "Is this how it always feels?"

Jane laughed her delightful bell-like laugh. "Every-single-time. Why don't you accept it for what it is: a great way for you to connect to the public?"

"I'm starting to wonder whether I made the right choice in coming," Dani said. "Being an introvert doesn't help."

"Better get used to it, darling. People are going to

want to talk to you. It's not all about the work, y'know?"

"I'm not used to being the center of attention."

"You're too modest. You must learn to revel in it."

"Just nervous, I guess."

"Pish-posh. What good is a painting if no one gets to see it?" Jane paused. "I should tell you, the show's a big success. We've practically sold out."

Dani's mouth fell open. "What? You're kidding? All the paintings?"

Jane laughed again. "Yes, all of them. Congratulations. I had planned to tell you after the show, but why wait? You're a runaway success, Dani Kowalski. Well done"

"I can't believe it," Dani said, shaking her head.

It was then she noticed an odd, little man at the end of the gallery, dressed in a dark, single-breasted suit, with a silver, satin tie and matching pocket-chief.

"Jane, who's that man? He's been looking at that painting for a long time." Dani had made a mental note, seeing most people only stopped for say ten seconds.

Jane took her eyeglasses from her purse. "Oh, that's Luis Delfin. He's an art critic. He writes stories for the Miami Herald. Very influential, darling. You'll want to get on his good side. Ah—don't look now, here he comes."

"Jane, great to see you! You're looking as radiant as ever."

"Oh, Luis," Jane said, with a dismissive gesture. "You're too much."

"Very sorry to hear the news about Helen Werner," he said, frowning.

"Thank you," Jane said, with a somber tone. "It

was a shock to us all. The gallery will start a memorial trust in her honor, with a view of donating the proceeds to charity."

"An excellent idea," Luis said. "You'll have to tell me where to send the check. But how shocking to think this could happen in our community."

"Yes," Jane agreed. "We were all stunned."

A waiter came by carrying a tray of hors d'oeuvres. Luis picked one out and tried it.

"Have you met Dani?" Jane said, changing the subject. Dani extended her hand and Luis shook it. "This is the artist whose work you were just admiring."

"Arr," he said. "So, you're the one we've come to see?"

Dani blushed. "I'm flattered you appreciate my work."

"Modest as well as talented," Luis exclaimed. "Très bien! Have you been painting long?"

"This is my first exhibition," Dani said.

"Extraordinary. Did you come up with a title for that one?" pointing.

"It's as yet untitled."

"Best to come up with a title soon. I think you're going to be a star. Work of this standard…I think we would all do well to keep an eye on you."

Dani blushed. The waiter came this time with a drinks tray. They all took a glass.

"Here's mud in your eye," Luis said, making a toast, and they all clinked glasses. Afterwards, he made a satisfied—*Ahhh*—sound and excused himself, saying he needed to mingle.

Jane also excused herself to speak with the exhibition attendant.

Dani noticed Eric standing by the reception desk.

He wore a gray sharkskin suit, with a navy shirt. Their eyes met and he walked towards her, relaxed, confident, projecting an air of masculinity.

"Eric?" she said, her voice rising in pitch. "I didn't think I'd see you here. Not after what happened."

"I couldn't stay away," he said. "I needed to see you."

"I didn't think you'd want to see me," her voice choked with emotion. "Not after all the things I said."

"Look, I know I was wrong. I shouldn't have kept that jewelry. I was waiting for the right time to offload it. You were right and I was wrong."

Dani sighed. "I think I might have overreacted. You were right. You had perfectly legitimate reasons for doing what you did. Will you forgive me?"

"Of course," he said.

She took his hand and squeezed it. "Jane said the show's a great success."

"I'm not surprised, Dani. Congratulations, you deserve it."

"I wouldn't be here if it wasn't for you, y'know?"

"I'm glad I could help," he smiled. "Say, what are you doing after this?"

"Probably trying to come back down from this cloud I'm on," she said.

He chuckled. "Would you like to get a drink with me?"

She nodded. "You bet."

31

Relaxing bossa-nova-esque lounge music played. Dani raised the glass to her lips, savoring the sharp taste of chardonnay on her tongue. A bottle of wine chilled in the cooler beside the table. Eric sat across from her, part of his face bathed in candlelight. For the first time in a long while, she felt like her old self again. To say she was enjoying herself would have been a gross understatement. In that moment, she could have purred.

"You're wearing my gift," he said, referring to the necklace resting on her breast.

"You noticed," Dani said, caressing it fondly.

He smiled. "You look beautiful."

Dani sipped from her glass. "You make me feel beautiful." She appreciated the attention. Lately she'd been feeling too much like the grieving widow.

Miguel's was a compact and sophisticated eatery, located on Fifteenth Street. She had considered various nightspots but decided on Miguel's. It had waterside views, and was the type of small family place where everyone minded their business. They sat inside rather than on the terrace. It wouldn't do to be spotted having a romantic dinner with Eric so soon after Chip's passing. Admittedly, she didn't know a lot of people, but that didn't stop her worrying. She worried someone might recognize her, but wasn't that part of the appeal? Part of what turned her on? It was taboo and it thrilled her.

It was a hot night, although a cool breeze blew in through the window. The ice in their mineral water melted, leaving beads of condensation on their glasses.

The customers at the other tables talked among themselves. Dani felt for an instant like they could've been talking about her. She strained her hearing. In her imagination, she could've sworn she heard her name spoken, over the hum and clinking of silverware.

A waiter came to their table and served their meals. They both had the shellfish bisque, and potted clams for starters. For a main, Eric had the rib-eye steak with bitter grilled radicchio, while Dani had the spaghetti pomodoro.

Eric took the dinner roll from his bread plate and broke it. "Have you thought about it?"

"About what? Dani said.

"You know? Key West. Will you come?" buttering his bread.

Dani leaned back in her chair. Of course she'd thought about it. She wasn't sure yet. All she was sure of was the way she felt for Eric, and she didn't want to feel sad anymore.

"I'm not ready to answer just yet."

Eric's brow wrinkled. "Concerned about something?" he asked, cutting into his steak, which was especially bloody.

"Well, for one thing…I know next to nothing about sailing."

He laughed. "I'll teach you. You'll love it…the unbridled freedom of it, the overwhelming expanse, and the star-filled night skies."

Dani swallowed. She still felt nervous around talk of the sea.

"Think about it…" he said, "the ocean breeze whispering the many secrets of faraway places. We can visit them all, you and I."

"And then what?" she said. "We'll get there fast and then we'll take it slow?"

He laughed. "Cute."

She smirked. "It's a wonderful dream…even if it sounds like it's from the back of a travel brochure."

"So, why not say yes?"

"It's not an easy decision."

"Think about it: you, me, plenty of sunshine, clear water…white sand beaches."

"It sounds great, it does, but it's not that simple."

"Swimming and sunbathing…" he continued.

"We can't," she said.

"Say yes. I'll show you paradise." He took her hand in his. "We'll stop at different ports, dine out, and wear the finest clothes. We'll worship the sun."

Dani smiled.

A waitress hurried from the kitchen, and the door swung, releasing a blend of heady aromas. The clamor of pots and cooks yelling momentarily drowned out what Eric was saying. Dani glimpsed an aproned chef lower a lobster, bound and tied, into a boiling pot, with a hiss of steam.

"I can't, Eric. I want to, I do, but…"

"Is it me?" he asked. "Don't you love me?"

Dani looked down at her empty hands. Bubbles

gurgled in a nearby lobster tank. She'd heard the question but couldn't bring herself to respond. She'd been trying to answer that question herself for days. Did she love Eric?

"Are you okay? he asked.

A school of tropical fish stared blankly at her from the saltwater aquarium by the wall. "I need more time, okay?"

Eric squeezed her hand. "I understand."

32

After their meal, Dani and Eric began the walk back to the marina. It was a nice night, a gentle breeze was blowing, and the Boulevard was crowded with people. Chance bits of music could be heard playing from the procession of cars driving the palm-lined street.

"Dani?" a voice said. "What are you doing here?"

It was Beth, dressed in plum-colored, full lace, and black pumps. She was on her way somewhere.

"Hey," Dani said, stopping midstride. "I guess I could ask you the same thing."

"I'm here with Matteo. He's parking—And you are?" Beth asked, looking at Eric.

He offered his hand. "Eric Gilman."

"Nice to meet you," Beth said.

An awkward pause passed between them.

"We've just had dinner at Miguel's. Do you know it?" Dani asked.

Beth shook her head. "Any good?"

"Quality food. Great atmosphere. It was nice. We're heading back to Eric's for a nightcap."

"A nightcap, huh?" Beth raised a brow.

Beth moved aside as a family ambled past with

their twin toddlers. The girl toddler—*ooh'd and ahh'd*—at a *Finding Nemo* balloon on the end of a string.

"Eric lives aboard his yacht," Dani said. "Can you believe it? It's moored at the marina."

"Really? What's that like?"

"It's comfortable," Eric said, "and cheaper than living in an apartment."

There came a rattling sound. A spray paint artist sat cross-legged on the pavement, shaking his spray cans, creating a realistic seascape on a cardboard canvas.

"So, where are you from, Eric?" Beth asked.

"Oh, here and there. I'm a citizen of the world."

"What brings you to Lauderdale?"

"Business. I'm an art dealer," he said. "But also pleasure."

Beth tilted her head.

"You know," he added. "The sun, beaches—"

"Nightcaps?" she asked.

There was a loud bang, which made Dani jump. Turning, she saw the girl toddler, red-faced and crying, her parents doing their best to soothe her loss over the popped balloon.

"Well, we better be going," Dani said.

"No problem. We still on for Thursday?" Beth asked.

"Absolutely—And maybe sometime soon Eric can take us all on his boat?"

"I'd like that," Beth said. "Even if I don't know how to sail?"

"That's okay," Eric said. "I'll show you the ropes."

Beth nodded and smiled.

"Ciao," Dani said, and the friends touched cheeks. She watched Beth go, and felt a swell of sadness.

"She was nice," Eric said.

Dani nodded. "She's the best."

She took out her cell phone and texted: *I like this one, Beth*, as they walked, and included a selfie she'd taken earlier, of Eric and her at the marina. *I was going to tell you,* she added.

"Who are you texting?" Eric asked.

She hit send. "No one," and they rejoined hands.

33

Beth spent that morning sunbathing and relaxing by the pool of her apartment complex. Later, she'd stopped at the best Cuban pork grilled sandwich place in Lauderdale. It was her favourite lunch spot and she'd challenge anyone to suggest better. Yet, despite this, she felt irritable. It was hot, and it took her ages to get ready for her date with Matteo.

They were having a re-screening of *The Princess Bride* at Savor Cinema that night, and Matteo suggested they go. She wasn't happy about it. She sensed something would happen on the way there, but couldn't tell what.

Beth often had these premonitions. She had a gift, the gift of the second sight, the ability to perceive the future or distant events. The moments before her spells were usually preceded by nausea, or by a tingling. She was often physically sick afterwards. Her nonna had the spells, too. She'd referred to it as *the knack*, as in having the knack to see things that others couldn't. Multiple generations of Tedescos had the knack.

Later, she had time to kill while Matteo parked the car and strolled the sidewalk. She stopped in her tracks, blindsided. Dani was walking with a stranger—holding hands no less. She could tell from their body language they were close, flirty. Beth bit her lip. *Why had she kept this from her? Maybe it was still new?*

"Dani?" Beth said. "What are you doing here?"

Dani and her mystery companion turned around. They had that deer-in-the-headlights look—that look people get when they're caught with their sticky paws in the cookie jar.

"Oh hey," Dani said, stopping midstride. "I guess I could ask you the same thing."

Dani was sheepish, bashful, and was giving her a look like—*Ixnay. She must be sleeping with him.* The stranger was handsome, but something about him wasn't right. His features were too perfect, too symmetrical. It gave him a sort of melted wax look. *This is so weird. Who is this guy?*

"I'm here with Matteo," Beth said. "He's parking—And you are?" Beth asked, looking at Eric.

He offered his hand. "Eric Gilman."

"Nice to meet you," Beth said. His hand was surprisingly cold and clammy, and he had an intense grip, to the point it ground her knucklebones together. She winced. There was a flash in her mind's eye and everything faded. A jumble of images tumbled through her brain: a stormy sea, a boat, and a web-clawed hand. She concentrated. There was a fourth image, but it wasn't clear.

"We've just had dinner at Miguel's. Do you know it?" Dani asked.

Beth shook her head. She felt sick to her stomach. "Any good?"

"It was nice. Quality food. Great atmosphere."

Dani said. "We're headed back to Eric's for a nightcap."

"A nightcap, huh?" Beth said, and was jostled aside by a family with twin toddlers. The girl toddler—ooh'd and ahh'd—at a *Finding Nemo* balloon on the end of a string.

"Eric lives aboard his yacht—can you believe it? It's moored at the marina."

"Really? What's that like?" She felt the shadow of darkness coming over her.

"It's comfortable," Eric said, "and cheaper than living in an apartment."

There came a rattling sound. A spray paint artist sat cross-legged on the pavement.

"So, where are you from, Eric?" Beth asked. She needed to know his connection to the images.

"Oh, here and there. I'm a citizen of the world."

Beth didn't like his answer. It seemed like he was evading the question. "What brings you to Lauderdale?"

"Business. I'm an art dealer," he said. "But also pleasure."

Dani furrowed her brow.

"You know?" he added. "The sun, beaches—"

"Nightcaps?" she interjected.

Eric gave a thin-lipped smile.

There was a loud bang and Dani jumped. The girl toddler had popped her clownfish balloon.

Beth watched Eric closely, while his head was turned, she noticed an odd set of creases on the side of his neck. *Weird.*

"Well, we better be going," Dani said.

"No problem," Beth said. "We still on for

Thursday?"

"Absolutely. Maybe sometime soon Eric can take us all out on his boat."

"I'd like that," Beth said. "Even if I don't know how to sail?"

"That's okay," Eric said, "I'll show you the ropes."

Beth studied Eric carefully. His eyes panned from Dani to her, and back to Dani again. His gaze reminded her of a predator's—unblinking and lifeless. It was unnerving, like there was no soul behind them, and something inside her, a primal instinct, cried danger.

"Ciao," Dani said, and they touched cheeks goodbye.

Beth looked back, briefly, as she walked away. The knack had come on strong and was sounding its alarm bells. She tried to concentrate again on that fourth image, but it wouldn't come.

She took a deep breath in. If Dani had told her she was seeing someone, she would've been there in support. But this guy made the hairs rise on the back of her neck.

Her phone vibrated. She took it out and found the text from Dani. It was a photo of Dani and Eric, by the water, embracing, with a smart-looking yacht behind. Her friend was smiling. Eric had his arms around her, and it gave Beth the chills.

34

"Hello?" Dani said, answering her cell.

"Dani, this is Dr. Buchinsky. I'm just checking in. You skipped a couple of appointments?"

"Sorry, Doctor. I've been busy."

There was a pause at the other end of the line.

"I heard about Chip's passing."

She bit her lip.

"I'm sorry for your loss," he said. "Are you doing okay? Do you want to talk about it?"

Dani cleared her throat, failing to keep back the tears. "I'm okay."

"I'm surprised you didn't want to talk about this."

"I guess I wasn't ready yet. Talking makes it real, y'know?"

"That's understandable."

There was another pause.

"Are you keeping up with the pills?" he asked.

Dani glanced around then looked at the ceiling. "I've stopped taking them."

"Don't you think this is something we should have talked about first?"

"I don't need them," she said. "I'm feeling better.

I'm having the dreams still, but I'm not anxious, I'm not scared."

"That's great, Dani. I think we should make an appointment, though, and we can discuss the medication in person."

"I'm not sure I can."

"Why not?"

"There's a chance I might be going away for a while, with Eric. We're in love."

There was a pause.

"I don't think that's such a great idea, Dani."

"Why, Doctor? I feel better, and more confident, than I've felt in years. I'm not nervous to go near the water anymore. I guess maybe the painting is working?"

"That's the thing, Dani, it doesn't make sense to have made this much progress so soon. Normally, it takes years of therapy for people to get over their phobias. Plus, there's this guy: Eric. You're just getting over losing Chip. And, I don't know...the way you talk...it has all the trademarks of obsession. I'd hate for you to make a mistake."

Dani swallowed. There was a tightness in her chest. "I'm hanging up now, Doctor."

"Wait—"

"I'll call you when I get back from Key West."

35

It happens again—you're back at the Ramírez house. Your heart is pounding. Adrenaline is pumping. Again, with your gun drawn...

"Police. Open up!"

You know you're in a dream; like an out-of-body experience, you can feel your actual self still lying in the bed of your apartment.

"Police!" you say again. "Come out where I can see you."

This is one of those lucid dreams; events flash through your brain like the flicker of images on a projector screen at a cinema, drifting past like a wisp of smoke. None of it is real.

You kick in the door and move rapidly down the hall. Your senses are heightened. There's a trail of blood.

This is your brain's way of dealing, you tell yourself. You've just hit that stage in your REM cycle. It's your psyche throwing up the mishmash of current events and past trauma—but this doesn't make it any less real.

You move up the stairs and into the final room.

It's like you are both the actor and director of your own film. Only you don't have any control over the scene you're in.

There's more blood—a lot of it. It's the girl in the yellow dress again. She's pale. Her stomach and all its contents have spilled onto the floor.

BANG!—There's an explosion of pain in your leg. You've been shot.

You whirl round and it's Ramírez. He's bearing down on you with a gun. Only he's different somehow. His eyes are wide and black, and his mouth opens impossibly wide, revealing rows of sharp, needle-like teeth.

"Fuck you, copper!" Ramirez says in a gravelly inhuman voice, leaning in to rend and eviscerate.

Frank awoke, shrieking, the sound reverberating. He grabbed his Glock 19 from beside the bed and did a sweep of the room. He felt vulnerable sitting there in the dark, with only one foot touching the ground, wearing only his boxers. For a second, every shadow and pile of clothes looked like a would-be assailant. He ran a hand through his damp hair. He was burning up. Sweat pooled in the notch between his neck and clavicles, and his heart thumped out a rhythm like jungle drums.

"Goddammit," he said, putting the gun back on its usual spot on the nightstand. He checked the time on his smartphone. 4:08 AM. Not surprising. It wasn't unusual for him to wake at that hour, depressed, afraid, feeling the effects of a nightmare.

Ever since Ramirez and the injury, Frank had insomnia and nightmares. He was used to long stretches without sleep, used to sleeping in fits and starts. He had to have a firearm beside the bed, too. If he heard a bump in the night, he'd confuse it for a gunshot. He knew it was crazy but didn't care anymore so long as he got some shut-eye.

This was the first time, though, one of his dreams had taken such a weird turn.

What the fuck was that? He grimaced. *Maybe I ate a bad burrito.* It was like Salvador Dalí had reached into one of his dreams and turned it into a surreal acid trip from hell.

Frank stood and wandered into the kitchen. He opened the fridge door, waiting for his eyes to adjust when the little light came on. The fridge was mostly empty, except for a wall of beer, several containers of moldy takeout food—left over from the Chinese noodle place down the street—and a plastic evidence bag.

He popped the top off a Budweiser and took a swig. *That'll settle my nerves.*

The bag contained that leather-like skin piece he'd retrieved from the Werner crime scene. Just looking at it unsettled him. It was odd. It didn't belong at a crime scene, and it certainly didn't belong in his fridge. *Why'd you take it home with you, you dunce? Just to satisfy your curiosity? What was it doing in that little dog's mouth anyway?*

He pinched the bridge of his nose, sighed, and took another swig of beer. "Fuck it!" he said, closing the fridge door. "Later I'll get Crawley to take a look at it. Maybe he can shed light on whatever it came from."

"For now, though—" He finished the beer, dropping the empty in the sink. "Time to get sleep." He was happy. The beer had done its job, and whatever loose end had been floating around in his subconscious had faded into the background, at least for the time being.

36

Albert was again at the espresso machine, speaking to a customer. "Yeah, that's the problem with young people today," he said, "they've grown up on a diet of TV streaming and social media. They don't know how to function in today's world."

Dani looked at him, bemused. "Don't you have some VHS tapes to unwind, grandpa?"

Albert chuckled. "Ouch. Too harsh, Dani."

"More coffee?" she asked a customer, who was making his way through a stack of blueberry pancakes.

He nodded.

As she poured, she eyed one of her paintings on the wall. She liked the piece. It had been a successful painting. It wasn't perfect, but she was proud of it. It was a testament to her burgeoning skills as an artist. She remembered when she'd painted it, the mindset, how frustrated she'd been with her lack of skill. It was all in the atmosphere, though.

At least her art was improving and people were taking notice. How far she'd come since the day Eric purchased that first painting. She owed a lot to him.

Beth had arrived and sat at the counter. She wore

a leather jacket, over a stripy shirt, with black leggings. They touched cheeks.

"Try the breakfast burrito," Albert said, tapping out the used coffee grounds.

"Okay, I'll have one of those," Beth said, removing her jacket and hanging it on the back of the chair. She cleared her throat. "So, it was a trip running into you last night."

"Isn't Eric amazing?" Dani said. "I like him a lot. What did you think of him?"

Beth grimaced and set her coffee aside.

"What…what's that look?"

Beth shrugged. "I just wasn't a fan."

Dani's mouth fell open. "Oh? What's there not to like? He's good-looking, he's interesting—"

"Call it…intuition. There's something about him that creeps me out."

"He's actually quite sweet."

Beth frowned. "He's—"

"Ladies, ladies, please?" Albert interjected. "Can you take it outside? You're spooking the customers."

"Thanks, Albert," Beth said. "That's exactly the word I was looking for. He's spooky, Dani. Your *boyfriend* is spooky."

Dani glowered. "Can I see you in private for a minute, Beth?" she said.

A moment later, they stood in the storage closet, a stack of boxes and personal items on shelves, a row of aprons hung on hooks.

"Why are you ruining this for me?" Dani said, with hands on hips.

"I'm not." Beth fidgeted.

"You are. You're being mean. Why are you being

judgy?"

Beth snorted. "I'm your best friend. It's in the job description."

"Not funny, Beth. Don't you care that I'm happy?"

"I care. I just wanted to be honest with you."

"Jeez, you make it sound like you're doing me a favor."

"I am," Beth said. "I think he's going to hurt your feelings...or worse. He's dangerous."

"Don't be ridiculous."

"How much do you actually know about him?" Beth crossed her arms.

Dani paused. "Well, he's an art dealer—"

"There. See? Not a lot, right? Isn't it too soon to be seeing someone right now, anyway—y'know, after Chip?"

"I don't see how that's any of your business."

Beth swallowed. "You should give yourself time to grieve."

"Don't even go there, okay? People grieve in different ways. I'm through feeling sad and sorry for myself. Eric's good for me. He's helping me move on."

Beth raised her eyebrows.

"I thought I could rely on you for support," Dani said.

"You can. I think you're just afraid to be alone, and...I don't know...it could be a self-esteem thing—"

"Shut up," Dani said, her face reddening.

"I don't trust him," Beth said.

"You're just jealous."

Beth huffed. "I don't even know who you are anymore."

"Fuck you," Dani said.

"Screw this," Beth said, and left the diner.

37

Beth stood in the waiting room of the Fort Lauderdale Police Department. She'd been in the queue, at reception, for close to twenty minutes. Rows of plastic, beam seats filled the room, occupied by anxious-looking people. A middle-aged couple argued about whether to bail out their miscreant son, while a young woman did her best to soothe a crying baby. It was a hot day and the automatic doors would open now and then, letting in a blast from the Devil's furnace. A large wall-mounted fan did little to improve the stifling atmosphere.

What am I doing here? Beth held a business card, slightly folded, in her palm. LT. FRANK HAGEN, DETECTIVE, it read. Frank had said, *'Get in touch if there's a problem.'* Would it be a mistake to involve him?

Beth dabbed at the perspiration on her brow. She had an obligation as a concerned friend. Dani was vulnerable after Chip's death, yet she rebounded with this guy, Eric, in no time at all. It happened too quickly. *What if Eric's dangerous?* In her experience, the world was full of users and exploiters.

She thought back to when she met Eric. The knack had hit her like a tidal wave. Its effects had left her nauseous for a couple of hours afterwards. She tried to cycle back through the images to interpret what they meant: a stormy sea, a boat, and a web-clawed hand. She couldn't piece it together. Nor could she work out what the fourth image had been. It was still, too, unclear.

At the reception desk was a tall policewoman with broad shoulders and a muscular build. She stood behind the glass partition, wearing the typical blue uniform, but with three inverted V-shapes on her shoulder. Beth wasn't sure what that meant. *Perhaps she holds a supervisory role?*

Beth cleared her throat. "I'd like to speak to Detective Hagen."

"Name?" the officer said, flatly.

"Bethany Tedesco"

"Do you have an appointment?"

"No, no appointment. It's a personal matter."

The officer thought on this for a moment before picking up the phone and dialing an extension. She conversed with a voice on the other end. "He'll be out in a moment," she said, hanging up. "You can take a seat over there."

Beth sat next to the mother with the gurgling baby. A news story was playing on the wall-mounted television, only it was an in-depth political analysis which didn't grab Beth's interest. She hoped Frank would help her. She had a gut instinct about him.

"Beth?" said a voice, a short while later.

It was Frank.

"What brings you here?" he said, flashing a

smile. He wore his confidence like a badge.

Beth felt an immediate attraction but pushed this aside. She was there for a reason and had to think of Dani. She wrung her hands. "It's a sensitive matter."

Frank raised an eyebrow. "I'll help if I can," he said, leading her to a quieter corner. "What's this all about?"

"It's about Dani," she said. "This is difficult to talk about, but she's taken up with this guy, who's a little...how do I put it...odd."

"Oh? In what way?" Frank tilted his head.

Beth tried to choose her words carefully. "Well, he appeared at Dani's workplace claiming an interest in her artwork? He sort of insinuated his way into her life. It's strange how quickly she's taken to him. She hardly knows him? He's not from Florida. I'm not even sure if he's American. He dresses well...he's handsome...but has a quality, a sort of aura. He's strange."

Frank frowned. "Jeez, Beth. I can't just arrest someone because you think they're strange. There has to be an actual crime. You know...theft, burglary?"

"I know," Beth said. Inside, she was torn. She wanted to tell Frank what she knew, but he'd think she'd cracked.

"You don't like him. I get it. We don't always like who our loved ones end up with. It's nice you're concerned for her wellbeing."

Inside, she was fuming. "It's more than that. I get a bad feeling about the guy—a bad energy."

"What would you like me to do about it?"

"I don't know. What if he's a crook or a rapist? Can you look into him? See if he has a record? Find out if he's on the level?"

Frank sighed and rubbed the back of his neck. "I don't know, Beth. We're not supposed to use police records for personal or unofficial reasons. It could get me fired."

"Please," Beth said, pressing her palms together. How could she tell Frank she was psychic and knew the guy was bad news?

"I can't exactly arrest a guy based on *could.* There has to be some evidence of wrongdoing." Frank loosened his tie. He put his hands on his hips. "I want to help you, I do, but if I followed every hunch...I'm already spread thin with my current case load. My advice to you is to try and get along with your friend's new beau. Try and see the guy for his good points, and who knows? With time, you might feel differently about him. Of course, if you get the slightest whiff of an actual crime, then...you have my number."

38

Manny sat at his desk, back at the station house, typing out a clickety-clack tune on the computer keyboard. "¡Qué asco!" he swore, under his breath. "You wouldn't believe the level of douchery on this *D8Swift* site, man."

Frank, who sat only a short distance away, leaned back on his swivel chair and chuckled. "You got some replies back, huh?"

Manny snorted, shaking his head. "You—would—not—believe. Want to hear this drivel?"

"Not particularly," Frank said, smugly.

Manny ignored him. (reading aloud) "'Hey, Sexy,' MrPerfect31 says. 'So, this might be random, but did you want to exchange nudes?'"

Frank sighed. "Can't blame a guy for trying, I guess."

"No, wait, wait. Here's another," Manny said, scrolling. "Hurton4u asks, 'If I ask nicely, can I lick your feet?'"

"Jee—zus." Frank screwed up his face.

"Right?" Manny said, rubbing his eyes. "I swear I can't take much more of this mierda."

"Any sign of our guy?" Frank asked, going over to Manny.

"Proteus? Nope. Nada."

Frank frowned. Looking over Manny's shoulder, he said, "I see you came up with a new handle?"

"Uh-huh, PartyGirl25. You like? The last one wasn't getting many hits."

Frank nodded approvingly. "Where'd you get the profile picture?"

"Huh? Oh, that's Anna Drozdova."

"Who?"

"You know," Manny said, waving dismissively. "Anna Drozdova."

Frank shrugged.

Manny stopped scrolling. "She's that superfine runway model from Latvia."

"Do you think that's smart? What if our guy recognizes her?"

"He won't," Manny said.

"What if he's...y'know...been to Latvia?"

"Stress less. I got this, mi amigo," Manny said, cuffing Frank on the shoulder.

Frank sighed. "I'm going to get coffee. You want?"

Manny shook his head and continued scrolling.

Frank had turned to leave when an electronic—*ding!*—sounded on Manny's computer.

"¡Hostia puta!"

"What?" Frank asked.

"It's him," Manny said, pointing at the screen.

"What...*him* him?"

"Si, gilipollas, who else? It's him. Proteus."

"You're shitting me? Can you print that?"

Manny nodded and somewhere a printer whirred.

"Well, what's he saying?" Frank asked.

Manny leaned in (reading), "'*Hi PartyGirl25, I like your profile. You're beautiful...*' yada, yada, yada. '*At the risk of sounding...*' blah, blah, blah, '*I wanted to reach out and see...*' He's asking her on a date."

A wide grin spread across Frank's face. "Bingo! Say yes already."

Manny typed a reply.

Three dots blinked on screen as Proteus typed. There was another—*ding!*—and a message popped up.

"What's he saying?" Frank asked.

"Easy, hoss. Give me a minute," said Manny, reading silently. He thrust his fist in the air, a moment later, and did a swivel in his chair. "He wants to take her to dinner—a place called *Gizmo's*."

"Do we know it?" Frank asked.

Manny nodded. "Not the best for a sting operation, but it'll do."

Frank smiled. "Set it up."

***

"Check, check. How's the signal?" Frank asked, tilting his head slightly.

"Loud and clear, hoss," he heard Manny reply, in his earpiece.

Frank scanned the dimly lit bar. Most of the patrons were sat on wooden stools chatting and laughing, laughing and chatting. Chilled jazzy lounge music played in the background. *Gizmo's* was a cocktail bar on Fifth Avenue—always bustling, with excellent food. It was where the corporate crowd liked to go to unwind. The décor was funky Americana, with vintage license plates and knick-knacks adorning the walls. It reminded Frank of a *Cracker Barrel* or *Ruby Tuesdays*. The bar itself was well stocked with lines of colorful bottles, and the air was infused with the fragrant smell of citrus and sizzling bar food.

He shifted in his seat. The tape from the wire he was wearing made him uncomfortable.

"I still don't get why I have to be the one outside?" Manny said.

He was parked in the surveillance van across the street, and already the normally affable man was getting surly.

"Because I have seniority," Frank said, covering his mouth as he spoke. "Plus, you drew the short straw."

"Yeah, well…next time we're on a stakeout you're in the van, and I'll be at the bar snacking on crispy fried whatever-the-fuck you've got going there."

Frank chuckled again. A passing waiter gave him an odd look, but he pretended not to notice, busying himself aligning the silverware.

"And how are you, Ange?" Frank asked, glancing over at a blonde who sat alone at an adjacent table. "Are we coming through, okay?" She wore a black figure-hugging dress, with knee-high boots, and her hair, a soft blow cut, sat in waves on her ample bosom.

"Crystal," Ange said, giving a surreptitious wave, before sipping her drink.

Frank gave her the finger-and-thumb OK gesture, disguising it as a stretch while yawning. Angie was a veteran Vice Squad cop, used to working under cover. He knew he could count on her when the chips were down.

"Nice of Vice to lend you to us, Ange," Manny said.

"Yeah, well…it gives me a break from all the pimps and the Johns."

Manny laughed. "Hey, you know those dresses you wear, Ange?"

She rolled her eyes at Frank as if to say, Oh no, here we go again.

"Where do you keep your gun?" Manny asked.

"That's for me to know," Angie said.

"¡Ay! Dios mio."

Frank shook his head.

"So, this guy calls himself Proteus?" Ange said.

"Yes, so what?" Manny said.

"Huh. Just interesting is all," Ange said.

"Interesting, why?" Frank asked.

"Proteus was the eldest son of Poseidon," Ange said. "You know…from Greek mythology? He was a sea-god."

"Get a load of Professor Brainiac over here," Manny said. "Ange, I'm impressed. You could be on Jeopardy or something."

"Alright, guys. Let's cut the chatter. Our guy could be moseying along at any moment."

"Do you think he's going to show?" Angie asked.

"Oh, he'll show," Frank said.

"Heads up, guys," Manny said abruptly. "I think this could be him."

The door of the bar swung open and a tall, muscular man, with coal-black hair, strode in. Caucasian but tanned, he stood a fraction taller than Frank, at around 6'5". He had high cheekbones, and an angular face, carrying a glassy-eyed expression. Through his button-up shirt, a bandage on his forearm was just visible.

"Speak of the devil," Frank said.

Angie saw him and waved, and he waved back, making his way to her table.

"PartyGirl25?" Frank heard him through his earpiece, the voice low, silky.

Angie smiled. "You must be Proteus?"

He nodded and sat down.

"It's nice to meet you," Ange said, without a hint of nervousness.

Frank listened. *Oh, she's good.* Ange was one cool customer, having met dozens of felons over her career.

"Ditto," Proteus said, before looking around.

"Nice place," Ange said, trying to put him at ease.

"You're early?" he said.

"Yes, well, that's me, Miss Punctuality. I hate being late to anything."

"Can I get you something?" asked a waiter stopping by their table.

There was an awkward pause as Proteus gave him a level stare.

"Umm, I might have another of these," Ange said.

"Certainly, Miss," said the waiter, accepting her empty glass, the words full of hollow enthusiasm. "Another Daiquiri for the lady. And how about the gentleman?"

There was another awkward pause. "Rum and coke," Proteus said.

The waiter swallowed, then went away to collect their drinks.

"I'm Lilah, by the way," Ange said. "What's your name?"

"You look different from your profile picture."

Ange coughed. "Um, it's an old photo." She smiled.

Frank leaned in. *Nice. Good save.*

Proteus smiled.

"So, what's your real name?" Ange asked, putting her hand on his. "Are you from Lauderdale?"

Proteus ignored the questions, glancing around the bar. Frank buried his face in a menu to avoid being noticed. Proteus withdrew his hand abruptly, stood, and made his way towards the exit.

"Arr, guys…he's leaving," Ange said, over the mic.

"Shit—he didn't tell us anything," hissed Frank, standing to follow. "Manny, he's gonna be coming your way. Keep eyes on him."

***

Outside, the sidewalk bustled with the throng of people: couples hand-in-hand; a lady in a crop top and matching yoga pants, lively speaking on her cell; beachgoers with swimsuit tops and cut-off denim shorts; and skaters wearing saggy pants, blaring hip-hop music over a portable Bluetooth speaker.

"Where is he?" Frank said.

"Eleven o'clock," Manny replied.

Manny had been keeping pace about fifty yards back in the van. Frank gave him a nod, narrowly getting missed by a car as he crossed the road.

"Asshole," said the driver out the window.

Frank waved him on.

"I see him," Frank said.

Proteus weaved his way through the crowd.

Frank kept his eye on the mark. *Don't you run, you fucker*. Proteus looked back, made eye contact, and quickened his pace.

"Son of a bitch! I think he made me," Frank said.

Manny swore.

"Hey!" yelled Frank.

Proteus glanced back then started running.

"Light her up, Manny," Frank said, giving chase. A short moment later, he heard the van's siren, and caught glimpses of the red and blue flashing lights reflected in the storefront windows.

Frank ran, his arms working back and forth like pistons, sidestepping pedestrians, his footfalls sounding heavy on the sidewalk. Bystanders looked around either confused or indignant. He heard Manny's voice once again in his earpiece…

Kish—"Calling all available units. We need backup. We have a plain clothes officer in pursuit of a suspect, traveling Northbound on Fifth Avenue…"

Gaining on the suspected felon, Frank drew his gun. "Stop! Freeze."

A bystander screamed and people scrambled to get out of their way.

Proteus cut left down an alley.

Frank holstered his weapon, while still in pursuit. Somewhere behind him, he heard the squeal of brakes, followed by more swearing. Manny must have realised the van was too wide to enter.

Frank hurried, the brick walls and balustrade on either side of the alley a blur in his vision. He splashed through a puddle, sending a glass bottle ricocheting. *Shit, he's fast. What's this guy on?*

The alley eventually opened to another busy street. Proteus ran in front of traffic to get to the park on the other side. Frank followed—again narrowly avoiding getting nailed by a speeding car. Proteus glanced back.

Yeah, I'm still here, you piece of shit. Frank panted.

Proteus jumped from the ledge to the park below. Frank followed—not sure of where he'd land—falling a distance of about eight feet into a garden bed. A throbbing pain detonated on impact at the site of Frank's old injury. He crouched for a moment, recuperating, before he took off running again.

Proteus ran, hurtling along a tree-lined path, nearly colliding with a couple of inline skaters. He reeled to gain back his balance before jumping over a park bench, through hedges.

Frank followed, bumping into a pedestrian as he exited. "Get out of the way!"

Proteus ran across the busy street into a pedestrian-only shopping mall.

"Where are you?" Frank heard in his earpiece. It was Manny.

Proteus darted into the nearby shopping arcade.

"I'm at the shopping mall on the corner of eighth and sixteenth," Frank said, nearly out of breath. "He's gone into the *Sunshine Arcade*." There was a hiss and a buzzing noise. "Shit," Frank said, removing his earpiece.

Inside, the brightly lit arcade, a world of glass and tile, a steady stream of shoppers occupied the walkways, quietly oblivious. Easy listening, innocuous music played over the mall sound system. Frank weaved in and out of the crowd, past lines of window displays, trying to keep up with Proteus. That's when it happened—a strange effect. Frank could've sworn he saw Proteus's face change. It changed to match that of a nearby shopper, an old man. The effect was uncanny. He looked like the old man's twin.

The fuck? Frank rubbed his eyes. "Hey!" He drew his gun.

Proteus turned, grinning at Frank with his newly-wrinkled old face. As he turned to move away, he was blocked by mall security and some uniformed police.

"It's the old man," yelled Frank, pointing, but the two cops and the mall guard didn't seem to understand.

Proteus darted for the nearest fire exit, setting off the alarm. Still with his gun drawn, Frank followed, kicking the door open. He was closing the gap on his quarry. Inside were several maintenance workers who cleared out quickly when they saw the gun.

"Freeze!" Frank said.

Proteus whipped around, knocking the gun from his hand. Frank dodged and countered with a punch, planning to sweep the leg. Proteus snatched Frank's arm from the air and lifted him until he was suspended over his head.

Surprised by this display of preternatural strength, Frank grabbed at the bandages on the Proteus' arm; blue blood seeped to the surface. Proteus grinned—with that old and wrinkled face—and heaved Frank crashing into the drywall.

Frank fell with a thud. *Jesus. What hit me?*

Still half-buried in the plasterboard, he thought about not getting up. Proteus grabbed him and pulled him to his feet, just as Frank snatched a wrench from a toolbox and struck him in the face.

Proteus grunted and loosened his grip.

"D'ya like that?" Frank said.

To Frank's surprise, Proteus grabbed hold of a support beam and nimbly climbed it, like a lizard, disappearing into the mezzanine level.

Frank's mouth fell open. *What the fuck are you?*

He found his gun and tore up the stairs in pursuit.

The mezzanine led to the adjoining multi-level car park. Frank caught sight of Proteus running at full speed. He jumped over a parking gate boom like an Olympic medallist.

"Hold it there, you freak!" Frank said, pointing his gun.

Proteus stopped.

Frank cornered him in one of the parking bays. Behind him, the Fort Lauderdale sky was a clear blue, and they could hear the mew of seagulls. Proteus' face changed again, this time to match Frank's. It was uncanny, like looking in a mirror.

"What—are—you?" hissed Frank.

Proteus grinned again, this time flashing a mouth full of sharpened teeth. With unnatural speed, it darted forward. Frank fired twice, but missed, the report of the gun echoing off the cement surface.

Frank felt like he'd been punched in the guts. Looking down, he saw a sharp bone protruding from Proteus' wrist, stabbing him through his torn shirt.

Proteus wore a puzzled expression.

"I'm wearing Kevlar, you, fuck!"

There came the sound of footsteps: two cops and a mall guard had arrived.

When Frank turned back around, Proteus had slipped over the ledge of the car park. There came a splash from the water below. Frank considered firing again, but Proteus had already disappeared.

39

"Where were you?" Frank said, back at the station house, his clothes wrinkled and covered with dirt and plaster.

"I was following you!" Manny said.

Frank kicked over a nearby chair. Several office workers looked to see the cause of the commotion, but wisely chose to busy themselves when they saw the fire in Frank's eyes.

Manny lowered his voice. "I couldn't get the van down that freakin' alley."

"Why did he leave the restaurant?"

"He must've smelled a rat."

Frank huffed in annoyance. "He was fast, Manny, damn fast—and I'm no slouch, even with this bung leg. And he was strong—like a weight lifter, or a freakin' circus strong man."

"He was probably jacked on PCP." Manny shrugged.

"The guy climbed a wall like a champion rock climber…His blood was blue."

"What are you trying to say, Frank?"

"Hell! I don't know what I'm trying to say." He

pinched the bridge of his nose, sensing the onset of a headache. *How did Proteus climb that wall? How did he change his appearance?* As a detective, he'd always dealt in cold, hard facts; he doubted the existence of the supernatural, but, now…

"This guy isn't human," Frank said.

"What?" Manny crossed his arms.

"Listen," he said, with a hushed voice. "I know how this sounds. Heck, I'm questioning it myself. Even saying it out loud… But I saw—"

"You saw what?"

Frank leaned in. "I almost caught him in that shopping arcade, but he ran into the crowd. That's when I saw him change."

"What do you mean *change*?"

"Like special effects in a fucking movie. His face changed."

"Bullshit," Manny said.

"No, I mean it. One minute he looked like the guy who walked in the restaurant, then his face changed and he looked like someone else entirely."

"You're having me on?" Manny said, putting a hand on Frank's shoulder. "Did you bang your head when you were chasing him?"

"I'm not joking." Frank brushed his friend's hand away. "I wish I were, but I'm not. I saw it happen with my own eyes."

"Aw, c'mon, there has to be a rational explanation."

"The guy had a knife, too, but it looked like a piece of bone, and it came out of his wrist like a damned switchblade. He tried to stick me with it." Franked showed Manny the tear in his shirt. "Heck, the bastard swam away from the crime scene like a fish."

Manny raised an eyebrow.

"It was real, Manny, I swear on my mother's grave. Heck, I swear on the souls of my unborn children."

"Dios nos salve," Manny said, crossing himself. "You gonna tell me we're dealing with some kind of shape-shifting devil?"

"Call it what you like, but this guy ain't human."

Manny looked down and shook his head. "My abuela used to tell us stories of the nagual when I was a 'lidl el niño—these are like witches, skin-walkers."

Frank nodded. "This is some bad business."

"So, what do we do?" asked Manny. "Do we call a priest, an exorcist…friggin' Ghost Busters, what?"

"I don't know, but I think we blew it. We might've lost our only chance to catch this guy."

"Aw, come now, I don't think we should be too harsh on ourselves, mi amigo."

"We had him in our grasp, Manny. We could've had him."

The trap was set. He just smelled a rat."

Frank batted over a jar of stationery, sending the papers on his desk flying. "That doesn't help his next victims."

Manny frowned.

Frank sat and put his head in his hands.

"Maybe if we put another ad on the Date Swift?" Manny said.

Frank swivelled in his chair, absentmindedly flicking through old case files, then stopped. "Wait a minute." A word jumped at him from the page like a rabbit on fire. "What did Ange say Proteus meant again?"

Manny shrugged. "It's Greek mythology. He was a sea-god, right?"

Frank showed Manny the paper.

"What? What am I looking at?"

"Look," Frank said. "This is a list of people who came forward with information about the Mandy James case. Do any of those names strike you as unusual?"

Manny leaned in. "No."

"This one," Frank said, pointing. "He's an art dealer right here in Lauderdale: Eric *Gilman.*"

"So?" Manny said. "If you know something, why don't you come right out and say it?"

Frank smiled. "Don't you see? Gilman? As in...Gill-man? Our unsub has a thing about the sea, right? He calls himself Proteus. We know serial killers often insert themselves into investigations. They sometimes even give supporting evidence. What if Proteus has done that here with Mandy James's murder?" He tutted. "Gill-man. Seems our guy has a sense of humor."

"I don't know, hoss. Seems like a stretch."

Frank shrugged. "What the hell else are we going to do?"

"Fine," Manny said, "let's bring in this art dealer for questioning, but don't blame me if it turns out to be a dead end."

40

Dani luxuriated in a bubble bath, in her Dorland Park home. Scented candles flickered in strategic points around the room. She used soap and a washcloth on her body, neck, and arms.

Eric sat on the edge of the bathtub with a towel wrapped around his waist, a glass of wine in his hand. He watched her. "You're enjoying that, I see?"

"I am," she cooed, and sank back into the steaming hot water. "Why don't you hop in here with me, good lookin'?"

He laughed. "I would, except I'm not really a bath kind of guy. It makes my skin all pruney."

"Hah!" She took a sip from her wine glass. "A small price to pay."

He reached below the surface of the water and caressed her. She giggled and splashed water at him.

There was a brief pause. She eyed the bandage on his arm. "So, what happened again?"

"Oh, you know...I scratched it...slipped while doing boat repairs." He took a sip of wine. "Have you thought anymore about Key West?"

Dani tilted her head. She *had* thought about it—a

lot.

"I just need to know." He shrugged.

She bit her lip. "The answer is, yes…a thousand times yes."

He laughed, leaned in, and kissed her.

"I think I should tell you, though…" she added, "My therapist, Buchinsky, doesn't think it's a good idea."

Eric's lips tightened. "Oh? Why's that?"

"He's worried about me quitting my medication."

"You've been feeling better, though?"

Dani took another sip of wine, but it went the wrong way and she coughed. "I think he thinks you've cast a spell on me?" She laughed.

"Really?" Eric rubbed the creases on his neck. "Why does he think that?"

She shrugged. "I don't know. Ever since I met you, my phobia has sort of…faded to the background. I mean that as a compliment," Dani said. "You have a calming presence. And you're a positive thing in my life right now."

"Oh, good."

"To tell you the truth," Dani said. "He just doesn't want me to quit therapy. I think he has a bit of a crush on me."

Eric's expression darkened. "How do you know?"

"He's always been a little too handsy if you know what I mean. Is it normal for therapists to hug their patients? He hugs me at the end of every session—and each time gets a little longer. And I see the way he looks at me. It's shameless really. The man's married. So inappropriate."

"Should I be jealous?" Eric said, sitting again at the edge of the bath.

"I don't know. Are you?"

"A little." He gave her a sideways look.

She smiled and grabbed his towel, pulling him into the bathtub with a splash.

41

Beth walked into the lobby of the Horizon Centre, a grand-looking, high-rise office building in the downtown area, the—*tick tack*—of her heels on the marble tiles echoing in vaulted space. The area was lit by subdued LED lighting and was filled with bustling people. She wore a business suit and sunglasses to blend in. The building was listed as the address for Eric Gilman's art dealer business. She had to see it for herself, to verify if Eric was genuine, kosher.

"Hold it," Beth said, as the elevator doors were closing. Inside were a slightly miffed, blonde woman, and a bald man in a power suit. "Sorry," Beth said, hitting the button for level twenty-eight. She cleared her throat and faced the doors—in line with the unspoken rule of elevator etiquette.

When the couple vacated the lift, Beth sighed. She was glad to be left alone. *What the fuck am I doing here?—I owe it to Dani.* People came and went in life, but Dani was a good egg, a true friend—they were practically sisters. She needed to protect her.

Beth was sure Eric was some kind of predator or charlatan. She had to prove it. The other night, her *knack* was trying to tell her something—but what? She didn't recognize all the images from her premonition.

She swallowed. There was a chance she might run into Eric. Thankfully, her spidey-senses weren't tingling. The elevator dinged. The doors opened, and she stepped onto the twenty-eighth floor.

What the—? Beth couldn't work it out. *Did I get the address wrong?* The floor was empty, deserted. There was a sea of gray carpet, and no furniture.

VROOM, VROOM, WHOOSH.

There was a cleaner, in a blue uniform, who was busy vacuuming. He had earphones in and didn't notice her.

Beth knelt and examined the carpet. There were tiny depressions where there had once been furniture. Over by the window, a mess of cables had been left behind, possibly where a bank of phones had been connected.

"Excuse me," Beth said loudly, trying to get the cleaner's attention. She tried again, waving for him to stop.

"Help you?" he said, switching off the vacuum, removing his earphones.

"Sorry," Beth said. "Is this Suite 'A'?"

"Yes," he said.

"Isn't this the offices of Gilman & Associates?"

"Gilman & Associates?" the cleaner said, giving her a questioning look. "No. Edsel & Morgan. They vacated yesterday."

Beth was dumbfounded and covered her mouth with her palm. She'd been right. Eric was a liar. He had lied about his business. *What else has he lied about?* She gazed out the window, trying to collect her thoughts.

"Miss?" the cleaner said. "Are you okay?"

Eric's a fake. "Um, yeah, fine," Beth said.

The cleaner shrugged and started with the vacuuming again.

Beth shook her head. *Dani, what have you got yourself into?*

42

"So, what is it?" Crawley asked, holding the evidence baggy between his thumb and forefinger. The pathologist sat behind his birch wood desk, dressed in his usual navy-blue scrubs. His office was the third floor of the Medical Examiner's building. On his desk, next to a novelty mug that read *"I only want you for your body,"* with a cutesy line drawing of a cadaver, was a framed photograph of the pathologist with his family, taken at the Magic Kingdom in Walt Disney World.

"That's what I was hoping you'd be able to tell me," Frank said, rubbing his tired eyes. "I figured it could be a piece of skin?"

Crawley looked at the object again, turning it over in his hand. "Where did you get it?" he asked, before taking a magnifying glass from his desk drawer.

"At a crime scene."

"I gathered that much—it looks degraded." Crawley examined it closer.

Frank sighed. "I found it in the mouth of a dead dog."

Crawley raised an eyebrow.

"It could be everything or nothing. Just a hunch."

"Did you find it near water?" Crawley asked.

"Why do you say that?"

"Because it's a little bit fishy," the pathologist quipped with a sheepish smile.

Frank rolled his eyes.

Crawley sat forward. "No. Really. Because, *to me,* it looks like animal." He handed him back the baggy. "Maybe fish or gator."

"How can you tell?"

"See for yourself," Crawley said, handing him the magnifying glass.

Frank did as the pathologist suggested.

"Do you see the little rows of jagged swirls?" Crawley asked.

"Uh-huh," Frank said.

"They remind me of the denticles you see when you look at shark skin."

"Denticles?" Frank asked, raising an eyebrow.

"Shark skin has this characteristic sandpaper-type feel because of these tiny dermal denticles…like miniature scales or teeth. It's like chain mail for sharks."

Frank scratched his cheek and nodded, taking this in.

"But I don't know for sure," Crawley said. "It's kind of outside my field of expertise. You'll need someone to identify it properly."

"Who could do that?" Frank asked.

Crawley formed a steeple with his hands, "Torrijos."

"Torri—"

"Dr. Luis Torrijos," Crawley repeated. "He's an

ichthyologist."

Frank stared at him, waiting.

"A fish expert." Crawley continued. "At the Marine Academy of Science in Miami."

Frank nodded. "Okay, so do you have a number for this Torrijos guy?"

"It should be here somewhere." Crawley nodded, opening his desk drawer, rifling through its contents.

"Ahh, here it is!" he said, handing Frank a business card.

Frank accepted it with thanks.

Crawley, looking back to the sample, "If anyone can help you with this, it's Torrijos. I should warn you though... He's what you might call an acquired taste. Highly intelligent. Just not a people person, if you know what I mean. An *odd fish*, if you'll pardon the pun."

Frank chuckled and looked at the card again.

"So, what's this all about really?" Crawley asked, leaning in.

Frank shrugged again. "Like I said. I'm acting on a hunch."

"Does it have anything to do with that Jet Skier that washed up on Central Beach? Or, that Harris woman?"

"Could be." Frank shrugged.

43

Martin Buchinsky lived in a luxury penthouse apartment in downtown Fort Lauderdale, within walking distance of Central Beach. He was late coming home that evening as, during the day, he'd had back-to-back sessions with patients, each just as needy as the next. It was tiring, emotionally draining work, but not without its rewards. He parked the Mercedes in the downstairs garage before coming up in the elevator. At his door, he tucked his satchel-bag under his arm, yawned, and turned the key.

"Honey, I'm home," he said, once inside, partly out of habit and partly to amuse himself. Eleanor was at a wellness spa retreat with friends and wouldn't be back until Monday. He slipped off his loafers and dropped his keys in a dish on the sideboard.

The entrance hall—like the rest of the apartment—had white walls, was well lit, and had polished hardwood floors. There was a mini-gallery of abstract paintings on the wall above a vintage cabinet, and a FontanaArte mirror dating from 1960. The overhead fans whirred, adding to the purveying feeling of claustrophobia.

Buchinsky took mail from the organizer atop the cabinet and began reading. Walking the length of the hall, he passed the mirror, his reflection thrown back, as if he had a twin. *Three bills and an invitation to a conference.* He screwed the papers into a ball and tossed them into the bin.

He set his bag on the walnut dining table, and removed his jacket and tie. The main living area was a circular room, with an ornate chandelier, an adjoining kitchen, a couch, and media wall.

The apartment was modern and well appointed— part of a former industrial warehouse that had been refurbished. When he and Eleanor had first seen it, three years ago, they weren't sure if they were going to afford it, even on their joint salaries. However, his therapy practice grew exponentially that year, and consequently, he was able to make an offer.

The décor was lavish—and why not? He and Eleanor could afford it. They liked to have nice things. Childless as they were, they were free to pursue their financial and career goals without the added pressure of parenthood. They chose not to have children for philosophical reasons. Eleanor believed it was inherently immoral to bring a child into the world.

Over by the stairs was a large fish tank where Buchinsky kept all kinds of tropical fish: goldfish, a couple of angelfish, tiger barb, a black phantom. He had read somewhere that keeping an aquarium could reduce stress and anxiety. He went over to it, took a pinch of fish food, and sprinkled it liberally on the surface. The fish swam and pecked at it gratefully. He liked fish. He liked the black phantom most of all. It had a black spot behind its gills, which made it seem like it had an extra eye, like the phantom was looking back at you.

Buchinsky went to the kitchen and checked the freezer drawer. Inside was the leftover truffle mushroom pasta dish Eleanor had left him.

Eleanor was an intelligent woman. She'd graduated top of her class at Columbia before going on to practice commercial law for a prestigious firm in Miami. She'd gone on the girl's weekend away to relax and catch up with friends. She deserved a break.

She's always thinking of me. He placed the meal in the microwave, hit the defrost button, and watched it rotate. Rubbing his beard, he tried not to think of the weight he'd gained since they were married. *I'll jump on the treadmill tomorrow.*

To one side was a home bar replete with an array of alcohol bottles, and rows of shelves all lit with colorful mood lighting. He went over and made himself a gin fizz. The soda hissed as he dropped in ice cubes from the mini fridge.

Buchinsky pulled back the curtains and stepped through the door onto the balcony. It was around dusk and the sky was transitioning from pink to purple hues. Between the buildings, he had a view of Central beach. He sipped his drink, observing the usual pedestrian traffic: a couple of joggers, girls in bikinis, and a kid riding a bicycle with a surfboard under one arm.

His mind drifted, and he thought about Dani Kowalski. *She's come so far under my guidance. It's truly remarkable.* He took another sip of his drink and listened to the sound of the waves.

He sighed. *She is beautiful, mesmerising.* He

longed to touch Dani's slender, young frame, to run his hands through her hair. *Why would the little seductress take up with someone else, though? Isn't she grateful? It should be me.*

The microwave beeped, breaking him out of his reverie.

Leaving the balcony door open, he came back inside, collected his meal, and sat on the couch. Mounted on the media wall was a seventy-five-inch, flat screen TV, with mini-LED tech and full-array local dimming—the best money could buy. He put his feet on the ottoman, took up the remote, and clicked through the channels until he found a rerun of *Frasier* he liked—the one about the Ski Lodge.

Having finished his meal, he set the plate aside and let out his belt a notch. A breeze blew in from the Atlantic, which bore the curtains upwards, twisting and dancing, translucent spectres on their nightly sojourn. Eddies of rich air cooled and refreshed him. Yawning, Buchinsky cast his eyes at the fish tank. All the fish happily meandered, doing laps behind their glass confines, except for the black phantom, which remained motionless, staring at him with its false black eye. Buchinsky thought this odd, but dismissed it.

The curtain rod thumped rhythmically against the doorframe—*Kaplunk. Kaplunk*—and Buchinsky promptly fell asleep...to dream…

Kaplunk. Kaplunk—sound the waves as they rush against the side of your uncle's fishing boat, a ten-foot dinghy with a modest outboard motor—not much more than an aluminium tub. But to your active 12-year-old imagination, it's a mighty frigate, and you and your uncle are the most feared pirates Lake Okeechobee has ever seen.

Uncle Sal has taken you fishing every weekend this Summer. You kid yourself and think, perhaps, it's because he wants to spend more time with his nephew. Deep down you know, however, it's because all is not well at home. Your mom and dad are fighting—more than usual. There have been arguments and throwing of household items. The dreaded "D" word has raised its ugly head. Your uncle is just helping out, keeping you occupied and away from home while your parents hash things out with the divorce lawyers.

Nevertheless, you're thankful for the time you get to spend with Sal learning about fishing. You admire him. A former Army Ranger, turned foreman for a construction company, his steel has been tempered in the fires of life; he's experienced danger and hardship. He wears a Miami Dolphins cap, chain smoking Marlboro Reds—it will be some years before the hospitals and before the cancer gets him.

It's a sunny, blue-sky day, and the light reflects on the water like a thousand shimmering diamonds. The dark waters of the lake stretch to the far horizon. A gentle breeze murmurs but still withholds its secrets. You have the new rod and reel your dad bought you. It's like the one Sal uses. On your last outing, you caught a large spotted bass, and you wonder whether you'll be lucky again.

"No, kid. You can't be squeamish about these things," Sal says, reaching into the bait bucket, retrieving an extra-large worm. "You gotta hold it like this." He held it confidently between his thumb and forefinger.

You eye the bucket of wriggling worms and grimace, before reaching in.

"The bigger the worm, the bigger the fish," Sal says, grinning.

They feel wet and slimy to the touch. They wriggle and squirm beneath your fingertips.

"Now what?" you say, having grabbed one.

"Now you gotta put the sucker on the hook. Like so," Sal says, deftly demonstrating.

You feel breathless and queasy when you see the point of the hook pierce the worm's gelatinous skin. It writhes and contorts. The blood drains from your face, and you manage to hold back the vomit.

"You try it," Sal says, with a nod of encouragement.

"Can't I wrap it around the hook?"

He laughs. "No way, you, goof. Just bait the hook like I showed you."

You blanch then shove the hook through. "How's that?"

Sal nodded approvingly. "Not bad."

"Then what?" you ask.

"Now we cast, dummy. Like this—"

You watch as Sal brings the rod back then quickly forward, using a smooth flicking motion, casting the line and tackle at least thirty yards into the blue. The hook and sinker disappear beneath the surface—plop!

You mimic his movement and do the same—yours doesn't go nearly as far.

"Good," says Sal. "Now we gotta sit and wait. Patience is the name of the game."

You nod, settling back into your seat. It's not even midday and you're already thinking about the ham and cheese sandwiches in the cooler.

A shadow passes overhead. You notice a cloud. It's about the size of your hand and it's blocking the sun. Within a matter of minutes, though, the cloud coalesces and expands, taking over the entire sky.

The clouds darken and you wonder whether this is a normal weather pattern for this time of year.

You turn to ask Sal, but he's fussing with something in the bow of the boat.

"Uncle, Sal?" you say.

Nothing.

"Uncle, Sal, these clouds— I think we should—"

Your uncle turns and faces you, but you notice something's wrong.

"What's that, dummy?" he says.

He is not the young man, fit and healthy, that you remember from your youth. Instead, his eyes are sunken, and his skin is sallow, jaundiced. He looks as you remember him, from his last days as a cancer-riddled patient, bedridden in hospital.

"What's that, dummy?" he says again, his eyes vacant, expressionless, dead.

His mouth opens wide, a sinister grin made up of rows of inhuman, needle-like teeth. You recoil in horror. In his mouth is a mess of wriggling worms. And it dawns on you he's been eating from the bait bucket. The juices from the worms run down his chin.

You scream.

"What's the matter?" he asks, coming closer, his face seemingly changing, morphing, becoming more angular. Uncle Sal is laughing, but now, it doesn't seem like he's really your uncle at all. His hair turns jet black—black as coal. "Don't you like worms?"

He holds a fist full of worms out to you, in one sharply clawed, web-fingered hand. You scramble away, but lose your balance, toppling overboard.

Buchinsky jerked awake, letting out a startled yelp, his skin clammy, his heart racing. He realized he'd been flailing on the couch like a drowning man. He ran a hand through his hair. *What a nightmare.* He hadn't experienced anything like that before. Certainly not in the years he'd been a therapist. He was usually the one to help people with their anxieties, with their recurrent nightmares, their night terrors. He'd never *personally* experienced them. He thought back to the details in the dream and remembered being *actually* scared, as if the threat of danger were real.

Strange. I've not thought of Uncle Sal for years—and he was different somehow. It was like someone, or something, had been wearing his uncle's face. He shuddered.

"Dammit!" he said, realizing he'd spilled his drink. He stood and set the empty glass aside. Another episode of *Frazier* was on television. He felt a chill. The curtains by the balcony still moved. Night had fallen, and the once pleasant breeze had turned frigid.

How has it gotten so late?

Rubbing his eyes, yawning, he switched off the TV and closed the balcony door. He glanced at the fish tank and did a double-take.

Something was out of place.

Taking a mental inventory, he marked the presence of the goldfish, angelfish, and tiger barb—but where was the black phantom?

Buchinsky started towards the fish tank, stopped

partway, and grimaced. He wondered why his socks were wet. Looking down, he realized the carpet was soaked. There was a trail of water leading from the fish tank to behind the couch.

What the—?

Something was wrong. He knew it but couldn't put a finger on what it was. He experienced a flash of intuition, a sort of nagging unease. Yet, despite his better judgement, he followed the trail, round the edge of the couch—slowly and haltingly—until the horror of what was waiting came into view.

It was the black phantom, and it had grown, preternaturally, to the size of an overfed rottweiler. The phantom's girth expanded and contracted with each pained breath, a great, quivering, gelatinous mass of fatty flesh and scales. Its demented, dish-like eyes rolled until they fixed on him.

Buchinsky reeled back and screamed.

Using its fins to drag itself, the phantom crawled towards Buchinsky, its mouth, and gill slits, opened and closed frequently, gasping for breath, trying to take in the non-existent water, revealing the red flesh within.

In his rush to get away, Buchinsky tripped over the ottoman and fell awkwardly onto his knee. A shock of pain went up his leg—he heard something go *pop!* He let out a sound like a whimper. Turning on his back, he was terrified to see the phantom still in pursuit, its groper-like mouth opening and closing in a chomping motion.

"No!" he screamed, close to tears, and he kicked at it.

It grabbed at his legs but found no purchase.

Buchinsky saw the face of the fish change and take on more human-like qualities. He recognised the face from his dream. It was the thing that had pretended to be his uncle. To his horror, it spoke, in a voice that was an inhuman gurgle...

"MA-ARTIN, DON'T YOU WANT TO PLAY? YOU NOSY PARKER. STAY AWAY FROM DANI KOWALSKI, YOU PAMPERED MORON."

Screaming and crying, Martin Buchinsky crawled as fast as he could down the hall. He didn't know where he was going; he just knew he had to get away. The phantom continued to try for his legs, mouthing and champing. He made it as far as the FontanaArte mirror before it caught him.

Oh god!

The phantom latched onto Buchinsky, working its way up his legs, biting and swallowing, consuming him whole—the pressure was excruciating. He shrieked in terror, trying to beat the phantom away with his fists. The phantom's face, a weird combination of both fish and human-like features, became clearer the closer it came to devouring him. Its eyes locked with his; the gleam in its eyes more than hinting at its devilish intent. Buchinsky turned his head, afraid to look at it. It was then, glancing in the mirror, he noticed something strange: the thing cast no reflection. When he looked back, the phantom was gone. Disappeared. Like it was never there. Had it been his imagination? Was he mad?

He lay on his back, sopping wet, and shaking with fear. In the morning, he would drop Dani Kowalski as a client. He wasn't sure what connection his waking nightmare had to Dani, but he wanted no part of it.

44

"Oh hey, girlfriend!" said a cheery voice.

Winnie Suarez grinned at Beth from over the top of her cubicle, reminding her of a meerkat popping up from its burrow. The twelfth-floor office space of the BCE building consisted of rows of cubicles and networked computers. Beth walked towards her desk clutching her takeaway coffee cup to her chest.

"Hey Winnie," Beth said, removing her sunglasses. She smacked her lips together, trying to rid a sour taste from her mouth. She'd been out late with Matteo and was starting to regret having not phoned in sick. "How was your weekend?"

Winnie brandished her cell phone. "Look, I took another photo of my girls."

Beth took the phone in hand. The image was a couple of felines dressed in matching outfits, headscarves with shades. *My girls* in this case meant Thelma and Louise, Winnie's two Long-haired Persian cats.

"Cute," Beth said, handing the phone back. "You know, though…usually…people who dress their pets—"

"Are awesome?" Winnie said. "Was that what you were going to say?"

"Not exactly," Beth said.

"You can't judge me, Bethany Tedesco." Winnie waggled her finger in mock derision.

Beth laughed and switched on the computer at her cubicle. She had a headache, and the sound of the office and ringing phones bothered her. She'd worked in the I.T. department of BCE Bank for the past few years. Great paid work if you could get it—spectacular views, too, if you didn't mind the fusty carpet smell and the soulless tedium. The little oscillating fan she had, by her nameplate, came on automatically and blew the loose sticky notes across her desk. She tried to catch them but only succeeded in spilling her coffee.

"Shit on a stick," Beth said, trying to use the sticky notes to mop the spillage.

"Hey Beth," she heard another voice say. She turned to see Larry Isles, one of the ethical hackers for BCE Bank. He was your run-of-the-mill, typical computer geek. He was curly-haired, rake-thin, and impossibly pale—for someone who lived in Ft. Lauderdale.

"Oh, hey, Larry. Your shirt is looking especially loud today," Beth said, referring to the Hawaiian shirt he had on.

"This old thing? Why thank you." Larry gave a florid twirl of the hand.

"Yes, truly another in a long line of bad wardrobe decisions," Beth said, winding him up.

"Ha, ha—So when are you going to stop ignoring this chemistry and mutual attraction we have and come to dinner with me?"

"Larry, leave the girl alone," Winnie said.

"How about…when pigs fly," Beth said.

"Harsh, Beth. Way to hurt a guy's feelings." Larry feigned dejection by clutching at his chest. "So who put the fly in your ointment this morning anyway?"

"Nobody." Beth propped her boots on her desk.

"C'mon," Larry insisted. "Tell us what's bothering you? You don't seem like your usual effervescent self."

"Effervescent? What's bothering me?" repeated Beth, taking her feet down. "I have a headache, and I'm hung over…"

"Getting hammered on a Sunday, Beth?" chimed in Winnie. "Rookie mistake."

Beth sniffed at this and went quiet. Which led Winnie to ask, "So what's up?"

Beth looked down. "A friend of mine is seeing this really suspect guy—I mean, I can't even tell you. Weird."

"Whaaat? That's terrible," Winnie and Larry in unison.

"I know," Beth said, "I bumped into them on Saturday when I was out with Matteo."

"Oh yeah, how was the movie?" Larry asked.

"Shut up, Larry," Winnie said, rolling her eyes. She wheeled her chair to Beth's cubicle. "Go on."

"I want to be supportive, but I'm struggling."

"As you would," Winnie said, leaning in closer.

"The guy she's seeing is just…"

"Just what?" Larry asked.

"Spooky," continued Beth. "She's only known him for a short time, but already has her wrapped around his finger like he's some kind of Svengali."

"Sven-what?" Larry said.

"Look, it doesn't matter," Beth said. "He's just creepy, okay?"

"And you're not imagining it?" Winnie asked.

"No, definitely not," Beth said, chewing her thumbnail. "It doesn't make sense for her to be so enamored. I think he's dangerous. I went to the address for his art dealer business, but the place was vacant."

Winnie and Larry looked at each other.

Beth felt sick. Her stomach pitched for the umpteenth time that morning. She thought back to the night she saw Dani and Eric. *He was creepy. That cold and clammy handshake. Those perfect wax-like features. Those lifeless, unblinking eyes.* Beth shuddered involuntarily. *How could Dani trust a face like that?*

"What do you think I should do?" Beth asked.

"I don't know...that's a toughie," Larry said, rubbing his chin.

"Let's cyber stalk him," exclaimed Winnie.

"What? Really?" Beth said.

"Yeah, totally," Winnie said. "Let's cyber stalk him. If his credentials check out...you can stop worrying about your friend, can't you?"

"Yeah, I guess so," Beth said.

"Good," Winnie said, rolling her chair to Beth's workstation, while simultaneously shooing Beth out of the way. "So what's his name?"

They all huddled around Beth's monitor.

"Eric Gilman," Beth said, hunkering beside Winnie.

"How do you spell that?" Winnie asked, typing it

into the search.

"I myself have occasionally partaken in some light cyber stalking," Larry said, "Mostly looking up exes and such."

"Oh, Larry," Winnie said, shaking her head, "Don't act like you have exes."

The color rushed to Larry's face.

"Here you go! Are any of these guys him?" Winnie asked.

Beth shook her head.

"Are you sure we have the name right?" Winnie asked.

Beth nodded. "Eric Gilman. That's what he said."

"Okay, and what about FriendPlace? Are any of these guys him?" Winnie said, scrolling.

Beth shook her head again.

"Don't forget ConnectSpace," Larry said. "Some people list their ConnectSpace name right in their profile…"

***

Winnie crossed her arms. "It's like the guy's a ghost. He's not anywhere online—besides his one-page art dealer business website, that is."

Beth frowned.

"Weird," Larry said. "Most people will show up someplace. Besides the name, do you have anything else on him?"

Beth chewed her thumbnail again. *Was there anything else? Had she noticed anything?* An image flashed in her mind, and she felt a sudden thrill of excitement. "The text message!" she said, searching her pockets for her cell phone.

"Text message?" Larry said.

"Yes, a text message Dani sent me," Beth said, still searching her pockets. "Funny, I didn't think of it before."

"Think of what?" Winnie said.

"Dani sent me a text message on Saturday night with a selfie of the two of them. Look, here it is," Beth said, flashing the screen at them.

Larry and Winnie looked at each other and shrugged.

"In the photo," Beth said, pointing, "You can see the guy's boat in the background."

"He has a boat?" Larry said.

"A sailing yacht," Beth said, nodding. She used her thumb and forefinger to zoom in on the photo. "And look here…you can see the name of the boat! The *Halcyon Daze*—days spelt D-A-Z-E."

"Clever," Winnie said.

"Can we search the boat name? And see what comes up?" Beth asked.

"I'm on it," Winnie said, already typing the name in.

Beth wasn't expecting anything, but she hoped.

"That's strange," Winnie said.

"What is?"

"It came up right away."

"What?" Larry asked.

"Some news story." Winnie turned the screen so they could see.

Beth had goose pimples on her arm as she read the article from months earlier…

Experienced seafaring couple, Ron and Margaret Dunlap,

who were holidaying on their yacht, the *Halcyon Daze*, in the Caribbean, are feared missing. Authorities reported they'd lost contact with the couple somewhere between St Lucia and Barbados. Search and rescue efforts—including two helicopters and five airplanes—started on Wednesday, February 12. The teams still hoped to find the couple and their missing yacht, searching until 5:00 pm Saturday, February 16. Subsequent searches also proved fruitless. Little hope remains for the missing couple. The searchers and family of the Dunlaps offer prayers for their safe return.

Beth looked at it, trying to register what it could mean. The boat…the stormy sea…these were images in her premonition. Below the article was a photo of an older couple. They appeared to be in their sixties. He was suntanned with gray hair and kind eyes. She was one of those older women who dyed their hair to cover the gray, only for it to turn a shade of blue. The Dunlaps were hugging in the photo.

Beth felt a heaviness in her chest.

"That's kind of weird, right?" Larry said.

Beth agreed. "Is there a way to tell if it's the same boat?"

"Now, c'mon, guys," Winnie said. "Cyber stalking is one thing, but are we actually suggesting this is the *same* boat?"

Larry shrugged. "Think about it. What is the likelihood two boats—of the same description—share the same name?"

"Exactly," Beth said. "Let's see if there's a *Halcyon Daze* registered to Eric?"

"Can't," Larry said.

"What do you mean '*can't*?'"

Larry said, matter-of-factly, "Well, even though

it's required for non-motored vessels of over fifteen feet to be registered, it isn't necessary to register *boat names*."

Beth and Winnie looked at him.

"What?" he shrugged. "I know a thing or two about boats, okay? My step-dad has a one."

"So how do we find out?" Beth asked.

Larry cracked his knuckles. "No problem," then wheeled his chair to his cubicle.

"What are you doing?" Beth asked.

"Just give me a few moments," Larry said, clicking away at his keyboard.

"What are you up to?" Winnie said, quizzically.

"Patience is a virtue," sang Larry. "I'm hacking into the DHSMV registry."

Beth and Winnie looked at each other.

"Aaand I'm in," exclaimed Larry.

"But you said—" Beth started.

"They don't register the *names* of boats," Larry said, "but it should still be possible to find the registration and make of the Dunlap's missing boat. Aha! Here you go."

She examined the number Larry had scrawled in his chicken scratch writing.

"What does it say?" Winnie said.

"That's the registration for the Dunlap's *Halcyon Daze*!" Larry said. "Also, it looks like their boat was a 2006 Hinckley Sou'wester 42-footer."

"So?" Beth said.

"So," Larry rolled his eyes, "all you need to do is match that number and make with the number on the hull of Eric's boat, and then you'll know for sure."

Beth stared at the number on the bit of paper and wondered how far she was prepared to go.

45

Beth paced the floor of Fort Lauderdale Police Department's reception area, hugging a manila folder to her breast. The same policewoman she'd seen during her last visit was at reception. The officer was occupied, filling forms, and Beth wondered if she really had passed on her message.

"You're back?" Frank said, appearing from a side door. "What's up?" His tie was loosened, and his sleeves rolled up.

"I think I have something here, Frank," Beth said, brandishing the folder. "Remember that guy I was telling you about—the one dating Dani? Well, I did some digging. It wasn't easy. The guy's a ghost. He has no online presence. No FriendPlace or ConnectSpace. Nada. Zip."

"Some people like to keep a low profile." Frank shrugged. "I'm not on social media. You should leave the detective work to the actual detectives, Beth."

Beth ignored the comment. "The guy's supposed to be a big, important art dealer, right? I went to the address where he's supposed to have his office. There was nothing there. The place was empty. It was leased by another business. The guy's bogus. He's a sham."

Frank raised an eyebrow.

"And there's this," Beth said, rifling through the folder before handing him a photo.

"What's this?" Frank said.

"Dani sent me that. It's a picture of the guy's boat. I had it enlarged. Do you see the name? I searched online and it turns out a yacht, with that same name, went missing at sea, several months ago—a husband and wife, who haven't been seen or heard from since. A coincidence? I don't think so."

"So, you're saying he's a boat thief?"

"Don't dismiss this, Frank," handing him the folder with the news article. "I took the initiative here. I know it's a stretch, but that's a heck of a coincidence, don't you think?"

Frank cleared his throat. "It's a coincidence alright."

Beth swallowed. *He's not going to help? He thinks I'm nuts.*

"I bet a lot of people have the same names for their boats," Frank said. "Nor would he be the first man to lie about what he does for a living to impress a lady. I need more than conjecture. More than hunches."

Beth frowned. *How can he be so obtuse?*

"Don't disrespect me, motherfucker!" came a stern voice from across the room. A large laborer had shoved a young Hispanic, and they were squaring up to fight.

"Step off, bitch!" the Hispanic said.

The laborer threw a punch, then the fight erupted, the violence spreading among others in the waiting room. The muscular policewoman stepped from behind reception and was attempting to break up the fight.

"Look, I better help break this up," Frank said, glancing at the brawlers. "Thanks for bringing this," referring to the file. "I'll take a look at it. I will. Can we talk later? On the phone?"

"Um, sure," Beth said. She thought she could convince him. She thought he was a better cop. *I'll have to do this on my own.*

46

Statement of Mr. Eric Gilman, [September 12th, 1:00 PM. Interviewed by Detective Frank Hagen]

Detective Hagen: We appreciate you coming in today, Mr. Gilman.

Gilman: Don't mention it.

Detective Hagen: No, really, I know these things can pay an emotional toll. It can be painful dredging up the past.

Gilman: Uh-huh. What can I do for you, Detective?

Detective Hagen: Well, we just need to—say, what happened to your arm?

Gilman: Huh?

Detective Hagen: Your arm. Why the bandage?

Gilman: Umm...I scratched it...slipped while doing boat repairs.

Detective Hagen: Right. As I was saying, we need to ask you some questions, again, about what you saw on the morning of Miss James's murder. Is that okay?

Gilman: Sure. Although I kind of already told the other detectives everything I knew at the time.

Detective Hagen: Absolutely, we know that. There are just some finer points we were hoping you can clear up for us. It shouldn't take long, okay?

Gilman: Okay. Shoot.

Detective Hagen: Shoot? That's funny...because we're cops, right? First things first...Your name is Eric Gilman. Is that correct?

Gilman: Yes.

Detective Hagen: Current address?

Gilman: I'm currently between homes. I live on a boat.

Detective Hagen: The one you're repairing?

Gilman: That's right.

Detective Hagen: You big into sailing?

Gilman: You could say that.

Detective Hagen: I think I detect an accent. You from Lauderdale originally?

Gilman: Not originally, no. I've moved around a lot.

Detective Hagen: Uh-huh. You married?

Gilman: No.

Detective Hagen: What do you do for work?

Gilman: I'm self-employed.

Detective Hagen: Oh yeah? That must be nice. Doing what?

Gilman: I'm an art dealer.

Detective Hagen: You must love it? I can't imagine there's a lot of money in that.

Gilman: Oh, you'd be surprised.

[Shuffling papers. Indiscernible.]

Detective Hagen: Okay, now that those questions are out of the way, we'd like you to think back to the morning you found Mandy James. It says here, in your previous statement, that, on the morning of July 13th, while walking, you saw a woman in the park accosted by a man in a ski mask, and you saw this from the nearby pedestrian overpass, correct?

Gilman: Yes, that's correct.

Detective Hagen: About what time was this?

Gilman: It should all be in my statement. It would've been about 5:45 am.

Detective Hagen: Do you always go for walks at 5:45 am?

Gilman: I was on my way to the store.

Detective Hagen: Oh yeah? What kind of store is open at 5:45 am?

Gilman: The bakery. I liked to get there early for the fresh bread. Plus, I like the exercise.

Detective Hagen: What was the name of the bakery?

Gilman: Huh? Oh, I can't remember. Sorry.

Detective Hagen: You said you were exercising. You keep in pretty good shape, do you? Are you fast? Can you run a mile in ten?

Gilman: Sure. I guess so.

[Shuffling papers again]

Detective Hagen: Now, it says in your statement, Mr Gilman, that from your vantage point, on the overpass, you saw a man, about medium height and wearing a ski mask, attack the woman, near the information kiosk? She screamed and fell. And what was he doing?

Gilman: He was sort of stooped over her. He had something in his hand—a knife maybe.

Detective Hagen: What did you do then?

Gilman: I called out for him to stop.

Detective Hagen: Did he?

Gilman: Yes, he took off.

Detective Hagen: Then what happened?

Gilman: By the time I got to her he was gone, and she was lying there, bleeding.

Detective Hagen: That's when you dialled 911, on a nearby payphone, correct?

Gilman: That's correct, yes.

Detective Hagen: You're sure?

Gilman: Yes. A couple of young joggers were there. They'll back me up. Are you reopening the case, Detective?

Detective Hagen: Yes and no. It was never really closed. There are some similarities between this case and another one.

Gilman: Oh yeah? Will this take much longer, Detective?

Detective Hagen: Not much. How tall are you?

Gilman: Why?

Detective Hagen: No reason. It's just...you're pretty tall, aren't you? We want to verify you could actually see what you said you saw from your vantage on the pedestrian overpass.

Gilman: I'm 6'5".

Detective Hagen: Ha! That's strange.

Gilman: What's strange?

Detective Hagen: I've been to that park recently, Mr Gilman, and I've stood on that overpass. There's no clear view of the information kiosk from where you were standing, unless you were like...7 to 8 foot tall, y'know?

Gilman: Hmm. Really? That's strange.

Detective Hagen: Yes, and so we're scratching our heads trying to work out how you were able to see what you saw. Care to revise your statement?

Gilman: I don't know what to tell you, detective, other than I saw what I saw.

Detective Hagen: And you're sure of that?

Gilman: Am I in trouble, Detective? Do I need a lawyer?

Detective Hagen: Do you think you need a lawyer? We're just having a conversation. Now, Gilman...Gil—man...that's an unusual name, isn't it?

Gilman: Not especially.

Detective Hagen: You ever do much swimming, Mr Gilman?

Gilman: What's that got to do with anything?

Detective Hagen: Nothing. I'm just making conversation. Have you ever been to the Blue Jay nightclub before?

Gilman: Can't say I have.

Detective Hagen: Can't say or won't say?

Gilman: I'm not sure I know what you're getting at, Detective.

Detective Hagen: Have you ever heard of a dating website called Date Swift before?

Gilman: Should I have? No.

Detective Hagen: Tell the truth. Have you ever used the name Proteus before?

Gilman: I don't know what you're talking about, Detective, and if you don't mind, I'll be going now. I just remembered I have an appointment to go to...and if I'm not under arrest?

Detective Hagen: No, you're not under arrest. You might say you're a person of interest.

Gilman: Why? Do you think I killed that girl? Do you think I did it?

Detective Hagen: I know guys like you, Mr. Gilman. You can't help yourselves. You're so damned wrapped up in your egos and impressed with yourselves. Do you think you can just insert yourself in a case? Do you think you can just get away with it? You're getting off on this, aren't you?

Gilman: I assure you, Detective, you don't know anybody like me.

Detective Hagen: Don't go leaving town. I'm gonna have my eye on you. I expect we'll be meeting again real soon.

47

It was late by the time Beth arrived at the waterfront. Moths danced in the lamplight of the dimly-lit walkway. Beth had come straight from the office. Working late was one of her habits, and the cab driver had taken numerous wrong turns. The marina was ahead, a series of yachts and floating piers, resplendent with their lights and glowing lanterns.

She couldn't be sure it was *the right* marina, but was reasonably certain based on its proximity to Miguel's restaurant.

Beth reached into her handbag for a lighter and lit a cigarette. *What am I doing here?* She took a drag. *I'd rather be at home, watching TV, with a bowl of mac and cheese, but, instead, I'm out here playing Nancy Drew.* She exhaled a jet of smoke. "Unbelievable."

She stopped on the promenade, and took another drag on her cigarette. Reading the news story about the Dunlaps, and their missing boat, had set her teeth on edge. *How can Eric have a boat with the same name? It's too much of a coincidence.*

She didn't like Eric, and she trusted him even less. *I'm going to find that boat even if I have to search every marina in greater Fort Lauderdale.*

The breeze rustled the leaves of the nearby trees. *If it's not the same boat, then…great. Eric will be in the clear. I'll stand back and respect my friend's decision. On the other hand, if it is the same boat? What then? I'll tell Frank. He'll know what to do.* She flicked her cigarette and stubbed it with her heel.

Creeping around a darkened marina in the middle of the night wasn't Beth's idea of a fun night out. Rich and fancy people moored their boats at marinas, which would mean security. There was a sign that said: PRIVATE PROPERTY, NO TRESPASSING. She typically didn't stick her neck out for anybody. *This isn't for just anybody, though. This is for Dani.*

She slowed when she came to the Dockmaster's Office. She eyed it cautiously, wondering whether anybody was inside, and as she got closer, she saw the light was on. The glass sliding door was open a sliver, so she chanced a peek. Inside, sitting behind reception, was a somewhat rotund security guard. He was reclining in an office swivel chair and stuffing his face with Doritos. An episode of *Brooklyn Nine-Nine* played on the wall-mounted TV, and the guard was laughing fitfully, in a high-pitched staccato way. *So much for the security.* Beth rolled her eyes and slipped past. She looked up, noting the CCTV cameras. They looked a bit too plasticky, fake.

Beth went along further, ducking under the chain that hung across the path. It gave her a nervous thrill of excitement. *I could get used to this whole Nancy Drew shtick after all.* The sound of the lapping water, below, the gangway, resembled little half-words of encouragement to her overtired mind.

The security was lax, it was late, and Beth bet that few boaters lived aboard their yachts like Eric. Still, she didn't see this as an excuse to go broadcasting her presence to anyone within earshot.

What if I run into a stray security guard? She wondered how that conversation might go. '*Miss, are you supposed to be here? Are you a guest of the marina?*' they'd say. *And I'd say something like, 'Well...um...you see...I'm visiting a friend.' No, that wouldn't fly.*

She turned onto the first pier. It was lined with sailboats. *What if I run into Eric? This would be difficult to explain. 'Oh, hi, Eric. What? Why am I taking down— Well, funny story.' No, it wouldn't go over great at all. I'm betting on him being out. If things get sketchy, I'll run away.*

She swore under her breath, doubtful she could tell the yachts apart. *What if I'm wrong and Eric's boat is at a different marina? No, it's here. I've got a hunch it's here and I'm going to find it.*

Suddenly, there it was—*Bingo!* The words *Halcyon Daze* were scrolled in bold cursive writing across its side. She recognised it even in the dark. The boat had green topsides like the yacht in Dani's text.

Beth glanced left and right. *It seems quiet enough.* The cabin lights were out, and all was still, except for the gentle rise and fall of the boat on the current. Eric mustn't be on board.

Carefully, she went to the stern and, using the light on her cell phone, searched for the boat's hull identification number. Beth had to stretch to try and find it, and it involved bracing herself against the boat with her free hand. Twice she nearly dropped her cell in the water. Eventually, she found it: a silver plate with series of numbers. It was right where Larry said it would be.

There was a splash in the water below. Beth dismissed it as the lapping tide.

She read the serial number. It included the manufacturer's code and the year of manufacture.

"Fuck," she said, as her eyes focused. "They're a fucking match. It can't be. Fucking fuck." She pushed back from the boat and almost lost her footing.

The serial number's identical. How? She took her phone and dialled Frank's number. There was a recorded message.

Shit! Voicemail.

"Frank, it's me, Beth. I need to speak with you, okay? This guy Dani's seeing…he's a bad guy. Anyways, we need to talk. Call me when you get this message."

She was so preoccupied with the onrush of thoughts she almost didn't hear the dripping on the pier behind her. There came the old woozy feeling that always preceded a premonition. Her *knack* was going haywire. Real alarm bells. Images tumbled through her mind: a stormy sea, a boat, a web-clawed hand, and…a fourth image. *What is that? Oh no.* She turned…

It happened in all of an instant. Her face warped into an expression of shock and puzzlement. Its arms lashed out in a rapid motion, stabbing again and again. She tried to scream, feeling a sort of wild panic and a desire to be somewhere, anywhere but there, but no sound came out. She sank down, blood spurting in a geyser, entire lifetimes slipping away, before…darkness.

48

The ichthyology lab at Miami's Marine Academy of Science was a white tiled room, with a concrete floor and fluorescent overhead lights. Its counters had an array of beakers, test tubes, and an assortment of complicated-looking, scientific equipment.

"So, what exactly is it you do here, Dr. Torrijos?"

The man in the lab coat adjusted his glasses.

He was lean, with an aquiline nose, and wore his beard in a goatee.

"It's what you'd expect. I categorize and study fish," he said, shrugging, "and other marine species."

"Sounds…challenging?" Frank said.

"It is," Torrijos said. "I write a lot of scientific papers. It's not for everybody, but it allows me to get into the field occasionally. Many of the samples you see here I collected myself, during dives."

The lab's shelves were crowded with rows of fish specimens, preserved in liquid: small jars filled with tiny baitfish; medium jars with elongated eels; large jars filled with all manner of Atlantic cod, salmon, and stingrays. It made Frank uneasy. Scores of dead, unblinking eyes stared from glass prisons, magnified and weirdly out of scale.

"On the telephone," said Torrijos, "you said you had a sample for me to examine?"

Frank nodded, handing Torrijos the evidence bag containing the piece of skin.

"It looks damaged," Torrijos said, raising an eyebrow.

"Don't ask," Frank said.

Torrijos cut a small piece from the sample and examined it under a microscope.

"Do you know what it is?" Frank asked. "Crawley said it had denticles—"

Torrijos raised his hand in a quieting gesture, before adjusting the focus of the microscope. Frank could tell the man's interest had been piqued.

After a while, Torrijos said, "It's an anomaly."

"Huh?" Frank said.

"A peculiarity."

Frank snorted. "I know what an anomaly is. Why is *this* an anomaly?"

"It would seem," Torrijos said, returning his glasses to their perch atop his nose, "that your sample belongs to an undocumented genus."

"You're kidding?"

"I never kid, detective," Torrijos said, flatly. "See for yourself."

Frank looked through the eyepiece of the microscope. "So, what am I looking at?"

"Do you see those jagged swirls?"

Frank adjusted the focus.

"Those are the denticles Crawley spoke of. Common in sharks. We are looking at some kind of marine animal. That much is certain."

"Okay, so it's shark?" Frank said.

"Well, no. Do you see those little dots?"

"Uh-huh. Yes."

"They're what we call chromatophores."

Frank looked up, his expression blank.

Torrijos continued. "Little pigment cells under the skin—they're used by some marine animals to blend with their surroundings, and are common in cephalopods, octopi, squid, things of that nature. It's rare for an animal to have both denticles and chromatophores. I've only ever seen it before in lantern sharks, and *they* live 1800 feet below sea level."

Frank blinked. "So, what you're telling me is, whatever creature this sample came from, it has tough skin like a shark, and can camouflage?"

Torrijos nodded. "Its skin would have small radial muscles allowing pigment sacs to expand and contract as needed, regulating the pigment and iridescence of the skin. This would help it match the surface textures of its environment."

Frank stood back, rubbed his face, and huffed.

"Are you alright?" Torrijos said. "You've discovered a new species. Aren't you excited? Where did you say you found this again?"

Frank bit his lip. "I'm going to tell you something and you're going to think I'm crazy."

Torrijos frowned.

Frank rubbed the back of his neck. "I came here today because I had a hunch. A crazy hunch but a hunch nonetheless."

"Go on," Torrijos said.

"I've been investigating several murders, which all share similar circumstances." Frank showed Torrijos some photos. "The victims, as you can see, were brutally murdered. Each had weird crescent-shaped bite marks and traces of marine animal venom in their system."

"Odd," Torrijos said, shuffling through the photos.

"You can say that again," Frank said. "Just last week, I got called to a crime scene. The victim? An elderly woman with a heart condition. She fled indoors from her assailant, where she was scared to death. Her dog had its neck broken. I found that piece of skin in its mouth. I figure maybe the dog took a chunk out of its attacker."

Torrijos stroked his goatee.

"For reasons I can't even explain to myself," Frank said, "I kept that sample out of the regular chain of evidence."

Torrijos listened intently.

"A week ago," Frank said, "we set up a sting operation to catch our main suspect. He'd been using a dating website to lure his victims. So, we create a fake profile and one of our lady officers posed as the date. Anyways, he must have smelled a rat because he took off running."

Torrijos leaned in.

"I pursued the guy on foot," Frank said. "He moved like the wind, and when I caught up with him, he picked me up and threw me like I was nothing. I saw him climb a wall like goddam lizard. He escaped by diving from a two-story car park, forty feet to the water below."

Torrijos' eyes widened.

"The weirdest thing of all, though...the guy changed," Frank said.

"What do you mean by *changed*?" Torrijos said.

"He just sort of morphed into someone else. His face and body altered until he resembled someone else entirely."

"Now, Detective," Torrijos said, rolling his eyes, "are you really trying to say—"

"What I'm trying to ask is…could a fish-man-hybrid exist?"

"Hah! Fantasy," Torrijos scoffed, but his brow wrinkled and he swallowed.

"What reason would I have to make all this up?" Frank said. "What would it serve? I know it sounds more like science fiction than real life. If I were you, I wouldn't believe me either. But do you think it's possible for some kind of missing link to exist?"

Torrijos chuckled. "Okay, Detective, I'll go along with the fantasy for a minute. Consider, there are 33,000 *known* species of fish in the world, and over 230,000 marine species in general. For every marine species we know about, there are at least four yet to be discovered. Is it possible you ask me? Not likely. Then again, man knows little about the sea in general."

Frank nodded. "My hunch is that's a piece of its skin. Which means it has…what did you call them?"

"Chromatophores," Torrijos said, with a sigh.

"Right," said Frank. "Would that account for it being able to alter its appearance?"

"Possibly," Torrijos said. "Animals will use camouflage for more than evading danger. Some predators use what we call aggressive mimicry, imitating their prey to avoid identification prior to attack.

"Makes sense," Frank said, nodding. "There's something else, too."

Torrijos raised his eyebrows.

"Remember I said the victims from these cases had traces of venom?"

Torrijos nodded.

"Well, before it dove into the water, it tried to stick me with—I don't know—a claw, or something? A piece of bone came out of its wrist like a switchblade."

"Interesting," Torrijos said. "Could be its mechanism for administering the venom. The hairy frog, for example, is notable for having retractable claws. Although not true claws. They intentionally break the bones of their toe until it projects from the skin."

Frank grimaced. "So, you believe me?"

"Oh, I wouldn't go that far," Torrijos said. "You're obviously delusional or you have an active imagination."

Frank's eyes narrowed. In his line of work, he wasn't used to being spoken to like that. *It's as if he hasn't got a filter.*

"I'll admit it's an intriguing notion," Torrijos said. "Look, I'm a man of science. I don't make decisions until all the facts are in. Can you show me where this thing dove into the water? Where it swam away?"

"Sure, but why? What are you thinking?

"I'm thinking maybe it chose that spot on purpose. It could be part of its regular range. Predators are habitual creatures, detective. Sharks patrol regular waters. I'm thinking I should take my diving gear and have a look."

"So you are going to help?"

"Let's not get ahead of ourselves. I'm still not convinced, but it can't hurt to look, and it's an excuse to get out of the lab."

49

Barnes stood in the department locker room, worn out and overtired. He checked his watch. It was late. His ten-hour shift ended over twenty minutes earlier, but he stayed to catch up on report writing. He sighed and wiped his face with a towel. Removing the radio and handcuffs from his utility belt, he placed them in his locker, next to the deodorant and extra mags of munition. It had been an eventful day, but not the most challenging he'd experienced. There had been a traffic incident in the morning, a three-car pile-up, a crash involving a fatality—but thankfully the paramedics were already on the scene; a DUI, a scumbag dentist who'd had one too many vodka tonics at lunch; some teenagers caught shoplifting at a 7-Eleven; a suspected burglary at the home of an elderly woman, who, as it turned out, simply had dementia and had forgotten she'd left the front door open.

"Hey, Barnes," someone said, over by the sink. Other cops milled around by their lockers.

Barnes sniffed. "Yeah?"

"Hope you got that old lady's number?"

"Fuck off, Gunderson. If I wanted to hear from an

asshole, I'd fart."

Gunderson shook his head and laughed.

Barnes removed his belt and hung his uniform shirt on a hanger. He still had his ballistic vest on, over his white tee. He reached to place his departmental sidearm, a Glock 22, inside the locker.

BANG!

Followed by a scream.

Barnes tensed instinctively. His heart pounded and his stomach backflipped. He looked to see if Gunderson knew what was going on. His pale face told him no.

Is this a drill? Then he heard the unmistakable—*pop, pop, pop*—of more gunshots. Quick. Loud. Spatter fire. He listened, his training kicking in. The space between shots, were clues as to the weapons being used. How loud were they? How far away? He pictured the department, mapping it in his head.

Barnes hurriedly put his utility belt back on. *Holy shit.* He racked the slide on his Glock, chambering a round. More sounds came from beyond the door. His mind raced, thinking it was terrorists.

We've trained for this. The Captain had made sure of that after a maniac with an assault rifle had attacked a neighboring precinct the previous year.

"Let's go! Let's go! Move it!" someone yelled.

Barnes and the other officers poured out of the locker room in rapid time, the outside corridor echoing with the sound of panicked footsteps—a typical formation, but panicked nonetheless. Dispatchers and admin staff ran every which way. The source of the commotion seemed to be coming from the main entrance.

That's when he heard it...

A strange whooping call that started low then rose sharply in pitch. It was like no other animal or man-made sound he'd ever heard. It chilled him to his bones, drawing water from a well of fear he hadn't known existed. The overhead fluorescent lights flickered and went out, while an ear-piercing alarm began sounding.

With guns raised, Barnes and the other officers moved ahead, cautiously, past all the plaques on the wall, past the noticeboard, then halted. The door at the end of the corridor opened, and through the gloom he saw a vaguely human-like figure. Whatever it was, it was tall, maybe seven and a half feet—and ugly. It had grayish skin, bulging eyes, and palpitating gills. Its webbed fingers had sharp claws, and its mouth was lined with piercing, sharp teeth.

My, god, what is that?

Barnes instinctively started shooting. The other officers opened fire, too. He felt he'd been dwarfed by an overwhelming presence—like a herd animal coming face to face with a lion on the Serengeti.

The officer at the front of the pack, maybe 15 feet in front of Barnes, had adopted a shooting stance and was still firing. Moving with freakish speed, the creature picked him up and threw him into a nearby vending machine. The officer dropped, crumpling into a contorted heap on the floor.

Gunderson lunged, hitting the creature on the head with a nightstick. Unperturbed, the creature turned, took the man's head in its web-fingered hands, and broke his neck with a sickening snap. Barnes saw the shocked expression on Gunderson's face before he collapsed to the floor.

Barnes swore and kept shooting. *How am I*

missing? I've nearly emptied an entire magazine and this thing's unfazed.

"Fallback!" somebody yelled.

Barnes and the other officers retreated while firing. Meanwhile, the creature kept advancing. Barnes dove behind a partition, taking a moment to reload. The cacophony of noise from the surrounding gunfire was deafening.

An officer tried a taser gun; two barbed darts launched by compressed nitrogen hit the creature's chest, delivering 1200 volts of electric shock. The thing bellowed and brushed the darts away, before clawing the officer, spraying the wall with blood, leaving behind a quivering, brutalised corpse.

More screaming and gunshots.

"Hey," a voice whispered.

Barnes scanned for the owner of the voice. It was Manny Dusola, hunkered down behind a row of cabinets. The detective was armed with a 12-gauge and was trying to get his attention.

Barnes gave him a reverse nod.

Manny held his hand flat over his head, giving Barnes the signal to cover him.

Got it. Barnes nodded, giving him the thumbs up.

Manny swallowed hard before he gave the signal.

Barnes stood and started shooting, while Manny broke cover, yelling, "Mother fucker!" Striding forward, blasting his shotgun repeatedly at the creature.

Barnes yelled, too, squeezing the trigger again and again. All the while he watched, in awe, as Manny charged. *The sheer guts and determination of the guy.* Glass shattered. Papers flew. Time stood still. The smell of gun smoke was heavy in the air.

The creature moved with almost imperceptible speed, dodging every salvo with relative ease. The creature seemed unperturbed, its toothy grin wide, its eyes unblinking.

Manny yelled, "Die you—"

"Look out!" Barnes cried.

The creature leaped forward, snatching the shotgun. Caught off guard, Manny went to draw the service weapon from his hip holster. He raised his other hand in a protective gesture, but the creature bit down, severing his fingers. Manny looked at the blood spurting and screamed.

The creature gave a savage grin, as Manny went pale, hyperventilating in shock. The face of the creature changed; for a moment it resembled Manny's face before changing back.

"Puta sin madre!" Manny said, spitting at the creature.

The creature roared, picking Manny up by the neck and smashing him into the ceiling light. The detective's head collapsed like an overripe melon.

Barnes whimpered, taking cover behind the partition again. All about him was confusion.

"Oh, god!" someone cried.

"No, no, no!" cried someone else.

Desperate screams.

His buddies were all messed up and bleeding. A wounded officer tried to crawl away, and the creature stomped on his head, smashing it like paper mâché.

Barnes crawled under a desk, panting, trying to stay as quiet as possible. *The holding cells! If only I can get to the holding cells...*

Barnes belly crawled past the interrogation rooms

and down the hall. The creature roared again, but it didn't seem to be following him. He came across the body of a downed cop, and grabbed the radio from the dead officer's belt. "10-999, I repeat 10-999. We have multiple officers down. The station house is under attack. We need backup, we need SWAT, and we need it now." There was only radio static. He grabbed the ammo off the dead man's utility belt and kept crawling. The holding cells were down.

I can make it. I have to.

He half crawled and half fell down the stairs. At the bottom was a swinging, barred door. Barnes used his swipe card and entered, making sure to lock it behind him. Beyond that was a sort of antechamber, with a desk set to one side, where normally the jailor would sit. *Probably left when they heard the commotion. I don't blame them. I should have left when I had the chance.*

He opened another barred door, which led into a long and skinny corridor with rows of cells on either side. Shutting the door behind him, he slumped against the concrete wall, trying to catch his breath.

"Hey, man. What's going on out there?" a voice said.

Barnes nearly jumped through the roof from fright. A familiar pair of tattooed hands stuck through the bars of the cell next to him.

"Zeke?!" Barnes laughed nervously. "You're still here? I thought your case was up for arraignment."

The other prisoners were yelling.

The hood was in an eight-by-eight cell with bars serving as one wall, and polished concrete serving as the others. He shrugged. "My lawyer took himself off my case. I'd even paid the slimy shit six G's. The guy lied.

He—Hey! You listening?"

Barnes ignored the man, slipping another mag into his Glock.

"Hey, let me out of here. I can help."

"Shut up," Barnes said, and licked his dry lips. He watched the wall-mounted security monitor. The image was poor and grainy, yet he could still make a looming shadow in the hall outside the entrance.

Shit. Barnes felt a sinking in his stomach.

The creature stalked forward till it was at the barred door, hesitated, then contorted its body so it could slip through the bars, like an eel.

The prisoners scrambled back into the recesses of their cells as it passed. They called for the jailor and yelled a laundry list of obscenities.

Barnes fired twice, forcing the creature back into the bars.

In a moment of pure adrenaline, Zeke rushed forward and stuck his arm through the bars, putting the creature in a choke-hold.

The creature roared in indignation, straightened, and snapped Zeke's arm at the elbow, before flinging the poor felon across his cell, into the opposite wall. Zeke collapsed, unconscious.

To Barnes' amazement, the thing transformed. Its visage changed to that of a man.

"WHERE'S HAGEN?" it said, in a gravelly inhuman voice.

"I d-don't know," Barnes said.

"WHERE IS HE?" it roared and turned back into the creature.

It grabbed Barnes and lifted him against the bars, screaming. Its jaws distended like a snake's, revealing a mouth filled with needle-like teeth, and it bit down onto Barnes' neck. The last thing Barnes heard was the sound of his own gurgled screams and breaking bones.

50

Dani leaned back in her seat aboard the *Halcyon Daze* and sighed. The early morning sunlight glinted off the chrome as the boat motored past rows of jetties and lavish houses. She listened to the creek and murmur of the boat, and the satisfying—*swish*—as the keel carved a path through the water, producing ever-widening patterns in the glass-like surface of the channel. Only the jogging crowd, and a handful of cyclists, moved about on shore. She marvelled at the sky, a masterpiece of florid colours, and struggled to remember the last time she'd seen a sunrise.

A breeze swept across the bow, helping to blow away the morning cobwebs. She wore the necklace Eric had given her, and fidgeted with its roughened inlays. Her suitcase was below deck, packed full of clothes, a handful of essential items, and her passport. It was all she needed to start her new life with Eric.

I'm doing this. I'm actually doing this.

It was as if she were in a dream. Her entire life had been leading to that point.

A trip like this is exactly what I need.

Back at the marina that morning, Dani tried to contact

Beth to apologize, to say goodbye, to explain. Whatever was said in anger would be forgotten. They were friends, after all. Only Dani couldn't reach her, and it was unlike Beth not to answer her phone.

She thought about it then dialled again.

"Who are you calling?" said Eric, at the helm, strong and sun-tanned, flashing a smile.

"Arr, Nobody." Dani sighed, putting her phone away. She arched her back in a stretch.

She loved Eric deeply. Her desire was unlike anything she'd ever experienced. There was the occasional pang of guilt over Chip, but her relationship with Eric was different, passionate. Already she was looking forward to their journey together.

***

"How long will it take to get to Key West?" Dani asked.

"Seven, maybe eight hours," Eric said, as the boat progressed to a different part of the river. "Depending on the winds, of course. There's a lift bridge ahead, so we're going to have to wait here for a while till it opens."

Dani nodded.

She looked at the fish-belly whiteness of her legs, and gawped. It always took her forever to develop a tan. *It doesn't matter. I'll sunbathe when we get to Key West.*

The bridge rose and Eric steered through the narrows into the wider bay. Lavish houses gave way to views of the city skyline.

As they passed through the heads, Dani looked back at Port Everglades, at the shrinking view of Fort Lauderdale. A lump formed in her throat as she thought of all she was leaving behind.

She took her phone—*Only one bar of reception*—and dialled Beth's number. *Shoot!* It went straight to voicemail again. Soon they would be too far from shore.

51

Dr. Torrijos was a competent diver with years of scuba diving experience. He had obtained his open water diving certificate in his early twenties and had snorkeled almost every day of his childhood, having grown up in a small coastal village in Panama.

Although he had explored much of Fort Lauderdale's inland waterways, he was unfamiliar with this particular bay area—the site where Frank had his encounter with the supposed fish-man hybrid. The detective had led him, convoy-style, to the spot that morning. They parked on a narrow strip of gravel running parallel with the shore. In front of them lay the blue-green waters of the bay. Crosswise was the concrete seawall, forming a tidal barrier. And behind them stood the multi-level car park belonging to The Sunshine Arcade.

Torrijos shook his head. *How could anyone jump from there, into the water below without breaking their neck?* Frank was clearly delusional.

Sure, it happens to cops all the time, he reasoned. *Their minds crack. They can't take the stresses of the job: dealing with the dregs of society every day, the societal decay, the violence. It must pay a heavy toll.*

In any case, Torrijos' first reaction to Frank's revelation, about a possible fish-man-hybrid, was one of pity, as well as mild amusement. He dealt in facts, not fairy tales. Nevertheless, he was grateful to be away from the confines of the lab. It was a beautiful sunny day; too pleasant to be spent indoors. Later, if anyone at the University asked, he would tell the truth, that he'd assisted the FLPD with one of their investigations. It wasn't the first time the University assisted the police in this way. They wouldn't need to know how outlandish the detective's claims had been.

Torrijos was already in his wetsuit, BCD, and flippers, and he had a flashlight with him. He shifted the tank on his back and looked over the edge of the seawall. There was a wooden ladder leading down to the water.

"What are you expecting to find?" Frank asked.

Torrijos spat in his diving mask to clear it. "I don't know, detective. Probably nothing."

Frank bit the inside of his cheek. "What should I do?"

Torrijos laughed. "I don't know…read a magazine? I'll be back in fifteen." He tried his regulator before entering the water and submerging.

The water was cool and inviting. He drifted with the current for a moment, waiting for the bubbles to clear. Shafts of light shone from the surface; their dappled patterns shimmered and danced. Alone, he felt the silence of the blue, the lonely rasp of his breath in his respirator. He adjusted his buoyancy and began his descent.

Despite the bright sunlight above, the visibility

decreased until he could see no more than twenty feet.

Torrijos was physically and mentally strong from all the diving over the years. What people didn't realize is how physically taxing it was. He was breathing compressed air, which is more difficult than breathing regular air. He was mindful not to hold his breath; otherwise his lungs would expand, increasing the chance of injury.

Checking the depth gauge on his wrist, he was already at thirty feet and still descending. Pinching his nose, he equalized his ears, clearing them out. It was getting darker and darker as he swam, so he switched on his flashlight. There was sand. Finally, he'd reached the bottom.

He kicked with his flippers, propelling himself along. The sandbed was carpeted with swathes of strap-like, shoal grass. He brushed this aside, and a school of fish darted in front of him. *I must be getting close to where Frank had seen the so-called fish-man enter the water.* He kicked again, keeping a steady pace. The bottom was getting rocky. The sandbed gave way to a rocky shelf and he changed tack, swimming upward. The top of the rock ledge had more shoal grass. Torrijos brushed this aside and checked his depth gauge.

When he looked again, he was shocked to see a face staring back at him from the gloom—a face with wide, unblinking eyes, attached to a body. His forward motion caused him to collide with it; the dull, spongy impact sickened and repulsed him. Reeling back, he saw it was a woman—at least, it used to be. It was white and bloated. One of its arms was severed, reduced to a stub of sinew and bone. The body was tied with a length of rope to a cement weight. Crabs scuttled across its skin, as it bobbed with the current, dancing with each ebb and sway.

Movement. As he swam back, he realized, with abject horror, there were more bodies. These, too, were tied and weighted, all bumping and swaying with the tide, a strange and unnatural harvest of fruit.

Torrijos' heart beat a staccato rhythm. He screamed, his mouthpiece shooting from his mouth, the sound a muffled gurgle, releasing a plume of bubbles. He reached for his mouthpiece, but couldn't grasp it. When he did, he forgot to exhale, drew in water, and gagged.

My god. What did this?

He spun around, scanning the water, suddenly aware of how vulnerable he was. *I should've stayed in the lab.* In a panic, he swam haphazardly toward the surface.

"Help!" he cried, kicking and splashing when he made it to the surface, realizing the absurdity of asking for help. *How can anybody possibly help? Nobody can undo what I just saw.*

He spat out his mouthpiece and removed his facemask, gasping for air. Suddenly, he could see the sun.

"Are you okay? Frank called.

Torrijos swam awkwardly to the seawall, before climbing one of the ladders.

"You okay?" Frank repeated.

Torrijos made it up the last rungs of the ladder, and over the seawall, before flopping onto the gravel, chest heaving.

"I-I saw something," he said, amid gasps.

"What do you mean?"

"B-bodies. Maybe ten or fifteen."

"Jesus!" Frank said, running a hand through his hair.

"What the fuck, Frank?" Torrijos said. "A human doesn't do that…A human doesn't behave like that. It's storing them. We've stumbled onto its fucking larder."

"You think?"

Torrijos exhaled heavily. "Salt water crocodiles will drag an animal under the water, and wedge it under a rock to rot for a while. Softens the meat. I think this is similar."

"I'll have to radio this in," Frank said, making to go back to his car.

Torrijos put a hand on his arm. "Wait! Tell me about this fish-man again."

52

Frank heard over the radio that the station had been attacked, with reports of multiple gunshots and officers down. Almost the entire FLPD has been wiped out. Terrorists was his first thought, but then he got there and witnessed the aftermath...

Bodies lay on the ground amid spent shell casings. A crew of firefighters were among the first responders. There weren't enough body bags to put all the corpses in, so they stacked them in rows in the station car park and threw blankets over them.

If this is the work of terrorists, where are their bodies? Wouldn't a firefight lead to casualties on both sides?

Inside, broken and dismembered bodies were strewn across the floor. These were cops, good cops, people Frank had known for years. The head of one of the victims leaned against a partition while the legs and torso were down the hall. Frank felt nauseous and stifled the urge to vomit.

This isn't the work of terrorists. Who could do this to another human being?

Manny's body was found with the others. His head

had been crushed, and he was missing the fingers of his right hand. Frank swore and punched a hole in the drywall. One of the firefighters shot him a look but knew better than to tangle with him.

Frank's hands shook. *I can't believe he's dead.*

"Frank?" said a voice.

He turned and saw a pale, skinny, bespectacled man with a goatee.

"Can I help you?"

"Linus," the man said. "From Computer Forensics."

"Oh, right, of course. You okay?" Frank said, putting a hand on Linus's shoulder.

"Better than some," he said, referring to Manny and the others.

Frank gritted his teeth. *How could this happen?* Anger and rage swelled inside him once more. "Were you here when it happened?"

Linus shook his head. "I was off duty. Same as you."

"I can't help thinking...If only I'd been here."

"Then what?" Linus said. "You'd be dead like the others."

Frank experienced a tightness in his chest and a wave of intense sadness.

"I need to show you something," Linus said.

They found Barnes, dead, down by the holding cells.

"Christ," Frank said. "They decapitated him?"

"It must've been where he made his last stand," Linus said. "They worked out who he was from his badge number, and his sidearm."

"He was just a kid," Frank said. "He had his whole life ahead of him."

Frank pinched the bridge of his nose, the tears flowing freely now. *Somewhere Barnes' mother and father would be crying themselves to sleep.*

"What the hell happened here, Linus?" Frank said, wiping the tears with his palm.

"I've no idea. We're still trying to recover the CCTV footage. Something interfered with the feed."

Frank raised an eyebrow.

"Could've been an electromagnetic pulse." Linus shrugged. "I'll let you know once we clean it up. Meanwhile, I know someone you might like to talk with..."

***

It was late by the time Frank wandered into Corwell Health Hospital, and the emergency room was in chaos. Victims of the Police Station attack, and an assortment of other accident victims, crowded the halls. After a quick word with reception, Frank headed for the orthopedic/ trauma ward in search of his man. Navigating the labyrinth of ivory-colored corridors, he eventually reached the ward in question and asked a nurse for directions.

"He's the one with the head injury, yeah?" she said, holding her clipboard. "Follow me."

The nurse started down the hall.

"He's in there," she pointed.

The room was dimly lit. There was an I.V. stand

and an oxygen saturation monitor that blinked and beeped. A single lamp light illuminated the patient's bed in the center of the room.

"Zeke?" Frank said, peering.

There came a groan. "Hagen? I wondered when you'd show. Am I dying?"

The hardened criminal wore a hospital gown, had a neck brace, and an arm in a cast.

"No, you're not dying," Frank said, with a wry smile, "but you're beat up pretty bad. A concussion. You were one of the lucky ones."

Zeke swore. "I don't feel so lucky. I feel like a truck hit me."

"That's why I'm here...to learn about the truck. Are you okay to answer some questions?"

Zeke shrugged. "I'm not going anywhere." He rattled the handcuffs, attaching his good hand to the bed rail.

Frank approached. Underneath all the bluster, he sensed Zeke was scared.

"What happened back at the station?"

Zeke glanced away. "You wouldn't believe me if I told you."

Frank felt a sinking feeling in his belly. Did he already know what Zeke was about to tell him? There was something off about all of this. Something supernatural? Something malign?

"Try me," he said. "Where were you when it happened?"

Zeke hesitated before beginning. "I was in my cell with the other inmates when we heard noises: screaming, yelling, gunshots. Coming from above." He swallowed. "It sounded like World War III."

Frank nodded, encouraging him.

"Argh—My fucking neck." Zeke grimaced, sucking in air over his teeth. He reached for a toggle beside his bed and pressed it. "This damned thing's broken," he said, referring to the nurse call button. "I've been trying to get someone in here for 30 minutes. I need painkillers."

"You *need* to tell me what happened," Frank said, glibly.

"I'm not saying another word till I get more drugs," Zeke huffed.

Frank went to the door and got the attention of the same nurse with the clipboard. "Do you think you can get him something for his pain, Miss?"

Without saying a word, she came into the room and checked the patient chart at the foot of his bed. Zeke gave her his best hangdog expression. She frowned. "It's not been long since his last dose."

"Anything you can do to help," Frank said, with a winning smile.

The nurse considered this before leaving. She came back a short while later with a couple of pills and water.

Zeke swallowed them gratefully.

"Happy now?" Frank asked.

Zeke raised an eyebrow. "Yeah. Happy."

"So, can you finish telling me what happened?"

"Alright—Keep your shirt on. Now, where was I? That's right. I guess me and the other inmates, were hoping they'd let us out, seeing there was an emergency."

"And did they?'

"Nope. No one came—despite all the yelling. Then

your boy turned up."

"Barnes?"

"Yeah, the young cop who was with you when you arrested me."

Frank leaned in. "What happened to him?"

Zeke's eyes narrowed. "He was terrified—wound up tighter than a jungle gym screw."

"Did he talk to you?"

"A little. Not much. He was preoccupied. He came in, shut the door, and stood there, aiming. I gotta tell you, it made the rest of us nervous as hell." Zeke shuddered. "I thought nothing was getting through that door, then...something did."

"Something?"

Zeke lowered his voice, glancing over Frank's shoulder to make sure no one was listening. "A monster, a real-life fucking monster. I'm not bullshitting."

Frank gritted his teeth. He had his suspicions, but hoped he was wrong. He didn't like where this was going. "Did you get a good look at it?"

Zeke went pale. "It was big, with grayish-green skin, and a mouth full of teeth. Then it *changed.*"

Frank's eyes widened.

"It fucking transformed," Zeke said, in a hushed voice. "It became a man. I kid you not. It just sort of morphed. I freaked. I couldn't believe what I was seeing. It was like an acid trip, or movie magic, y'know?"

At first Frank didn't understand; he didn't want to understand. *Of course.* It dawned on him. It was Gilman who had attacked the station. The pieces fit together. Suddenly he felt nauseous.

"What did he—I mean *it*—look like as a man?"

"I didn't get a good look at his face, but he was tall, with black hair—"

"Did it speak?"

Zeke frowned. "Just before I blacked out I heard it ask Barnes about you. It got real mad, too, when he said you weren't there. All hell broke loose."

Frank turned away. His stomach was churning and his hands were shaking. *Oh god. All those deaths. Am I responsible?* He'd antagonized Gilman to draw him out, but hadn't expected him—it— to retaliate. Not like this.

"You okay?" Zeke asked.

Franked straightened and coughed. He made a dismissive gesture. "So how did you…?"

Zeke laughed nervously. "That's when I had what you might call an uncharacteristic bout of bravery. Call it fight or flight—I don't know—I knew I had to do something. When it passed the cells, I grabbed it."

Frank raised his eyebrows. "You grabbed it?"

"I tried to put it in a chokehold. That didn't work out too well for me, though, as you can see?" referring to his injuries.

Frank took a couple of deep breaths, rubbing his temples. His head was pounding. *This can't be.* It was clear the creature—that had single-handedly taken down the FLPD, killed Manny, Barnes, and countless others— was the same one he'd tangled with at the *Sunshine Arcade.*

"You okay, detective?" Zeke asked. "You're looking a little pale."

Frank ignored him, too engrossed in his own thoughts to listen. He'd come to know the creature as Proteus, but more than likely that was an alias for Eric Gilman. It was responsible for a string of murders, including the bodies in the harbor.

What is it—a devil? He didn't know, but it was looking for him. *It knows I'm onto it.*

Zeke chimed in again. "Look, I was wondering...Will I get some kind of special dispensation? Y'know, for my injuries? The FLPD could at least foot my hospital bill."

"Look, thanks," Frank said. "I'll be back if I think of any other questions," leaving abruptly.

Frank got an alert on his cell phone as he was leaving the hospital. He stopped in the main vestibule to check the text message, and saw it was from Linus in Computer Forensics. They'd managed to salvage the CCTV footage from the station house. He drew in a breath as he clicked on the attached link. It opened to a video, some grainy footage of Barnes' last stand in the holding cells. One minute Barnes was okay. The next, he was being murdered, in the most unspeakable way, by a monster.

53

Frank knocked on the door of Doctor Torrijos' apartment and waited. There came the sound of footsteps.

"Hello?" came a voice, through the door.

"Doctor, it's me, Hagen."

"What do you want?" the door opened a crack.

"I want to speak with you. I rang the university, but they said you called in sick."

"Go away. I need to be alone right now." Torrijos tried to shut the door.

Frank put his foot in to prevent it from shutting. "I need to speak with you."

"Why me?" Torrijos said.

"Because you're the only one who seems to know anything about this *thing*. It's attacked the police station and killed countless people, including my friends."

Torrijos relented and opened the door. "You better come in."

Inside was fastidiously organized, compulsively neat. The books on the shelves were arranged by height and size, as well as color; the furniture was at right angles; and there was not a speck of dust. The blinds to the apartment were shut, despite it being during the day. Torrijos was pale with bags under his eyes.

"Tea?" Torrijos asked.

"Sure," Frank said.

Torrijos put the kettle on to boil in the kitchen. "I'm not sure how much I can help you."

Frank picked up a large conch shell from the sideboard to examine it, then put it back.

"Sugar?" Torrijos asked.

"Sure," Frank said.

Torrijos returned to the living room, a moment later, with the tea. Frank accepted his, cradling the cup to warm his hands.

Torrijos surreptitiously straightened the conch shell so it aligned with other trinkets on the sideboard.

"Please, sit," Torrijos said, gesturing to the couch.

They sat.

"You must know more about this creature," Frank said.

Torrijos sipped his tea. "Mr. Hagen. I've been a marine biologist for twenty-five years, and diving for thirty. I love it. It's my passion. But ever since the other day…" He sighed. "I've been afraid to go into work and the thought of diving fills me with dread."

"That's only natural," Frank said, "considering the scare you had—seeing all those bodies."

"It's more than that, detective. Seeing those bodies and hearing about the attack on the police station convinces me—more than ever—that you're dealing with something *supernatural*. This is no animal or unnamed cryptid. This is a manifestation of evil."

Frank tilted his head. "I thought you were a '*man of science*?'"

Torrijos waved this off. "That's just what I tell people. That day you came to Marine Academy, talking about a fish-man, I was skeptical. At the same time, though, I was reminded of a myth, a legend, from my homeland, Panama." He looked down. "They call him El Mohán."

Frank listened, at the same time wishing he had something stronger than tea to drink.

"I grew up in a small fishing village," continued Torrijos. "My grandmother looked after me and my siblings while our parents were at work. She would tell us stories to entertain us, and to keep us on the straight and narrow. '*You better behave, or El Mohán will get you,*' she would say. '*You better hurry and go to bed, or El Mohán will come.*'

Frank shifted.

"El Mohán was said to haunt the reef around Pedasi, in Azuero province—not far from where I was born—on the South-Eastern tip of the Azuero Peninsula," Torrijos said. "The locals knew this, so they avoided the reef. People would sometimes see his footprints in the sand. Other times they claimed to see El Mohán himself, but always from a distance. He'd either appear as a tall man or…as a fish-man."

Frank raised an eyebrow.

"The legend states El Mohán was the worst of the merfolk; a half-man, half-fish who roamed the coastline; a giant and cannibal, who was fond of human blood. Disguising himself as a man, he would seduce women from coastal villages. He would prey on them, gaining their confidence, bearing gifts from his hoard of gold, before taking them to his underwater lair—never to be seen or heard from again."

"And you believe that?"

He shrugged. "Well, I do now. And if you believe the lore, he's done it for generations. When my grandmother was a niña, there was a woman in her village who, supposedly, lay with El Mohán. That woman gave birth to a child covered from head to tail in scales like a fish, and a membrane between her toes."

Frank sighed, shaking his head. "Okay then, what is a centuries-old fish-man doing here in America?"

"Maybe it wanted a change of scenery, a different hunting ground? Killer whales migrate as far as seven thousand miles. Did you know that?"

"What does it want?"

"What do all devils want, detective—to deceive, and to hunt us for sport? Who knows? You say it can mimic anybody, and it can change its appearance? Sounds to me like we have a monster who's trying to be a man."

Frank frowned.

"It called itself Proteus," Torrijos continued. "Perhaps that's a clue. According to Greek mythology, Proteus was a subject of Poseidon, the god of the sea. He was described as being ageless and had knowledge of hidden things. If caught, he would escape by assuming all manner of shapes. Sound familiar?"

"He's been baiting us?" Frank said. "He's been dropping clues all along."

Torrijos nodded. "Why would he kill or eat these women, his victims? you might wonder. In many cultures there is the concept of the vampire, the cannibal that feeds on blood. I suspect he consumes their flesh to keep himself young, ageless. I suspect he also enjoys it, the sport of it."

"Okay, let's say you're right. If this thing is some kind of boogie man, how do we kill it?"

"We don't. The thing you need to understand, detective, is…this is no animal. We're dealing with a supernatural being, a sea spirit. It *is* the sea."

"Why don't bullets affect it?"

"Have you ever tried to hold water? Or, grasp a moving river? It's the stuff of dreams. How can you kill a nightmare?"

"But that patch of skin I brought you that day," Frank said, "I found it in a little dog's mouth. How could a dog take a bite out of it?"

Torrijos shrugged. "Perhaps it was still *a man* when it was bitten? Your guess is as good as mine, but, until El Mohán migrates again, I'm staying right here— in my apartment."

54

Frank was concerned. On top of everything—Manny and Barnes dead, Gilman's attack on the Station House—Beth Tedesco had left a cryptic message on his voicemail, and wasn't answering her phone.

He played the message back, for the umpteenth time in a row. He listened to the intonation of her voice. *Worried. About what exactly? She wanted to talk. It had something to do with the guy Dani was seeing. 'A bad guy.'*

Frank got sick of waiting. He left numerous messages but didn't hear back. He went first to her apartment and rang the intercom, but there was no answer, so he got the super to let him in. She wasn't there. He then went to BCE, to see if she'd been to work.

Going up in the elevator, to the twelfth floor, he checked his reflection in the mirror. There was a dark circle under each eye. He still wasn't sleeping.

The door of the elevator slid open, to reveal a large workspace with rows of cubicles. He caught the attention of a woman at the nearest desk. "Excuse me, can you tell me if Bethany Tedesco is in?"

The woman, with photos of cats all over her cubicle, looked more than a little troubled at the question.

"Can I ask why? Are you a friend of hers?"

Frank's lips tightened. He showed the woman his badge. "I'm a detective with the FLPD, but I'm here on an unofficial capacity."

"Oh," said the woman standing up, extending her hand. "Winnie Suarez."

Frank shook her hand. "Well, is she here, Winnie? I'd love to speak with her."

Winnie frowned. "I'm afraid not. She's not been to work for a few days, or even called in sick. To tell you the truth, we were getting worried."

Frank grimaced. "Exactly what I hoped you wouldn't say."

"We tried to file a report," a voice said.

"What's that?" Frank said, turning to face the man.

He was a pale, skinny, and dressed in a Hawaiian shirt, and his workstation was bedecked in Star Trek paraphernalia.

"I said we tried to file a missing person report, but the police said we had to wait seventy-two hours. Then that thing happened: the attack on the FLPD."

"A tragedy." Winnie shook her head.

"Larry Isles," said the man, extending his hand.

Frank shook it. "What made you want to file a report?"

Larry shrugged. "Beth doesn't have an emergency contact or family to call, and it was unlike her to skip work. But, there was this drama with her friend's boyfriend."

"Drama?" Frank asked.

"Beth's girlfriend, Dani, was seeing this really *weird* guy," Winnie said. "Beth said he gave her the heebee-jeebees."

"We looked the dude up on the internet," Larry said. "It was like he didn't exist. Real suspicious."

"Strange," Winnie said, nodding.

"So, Beth has this bright idea about looking up the name of his boat, the *Halcyon Daze.*"

"And?" Frank said.

"Alarm bells," Larry said. "Turns out a boat by the same name went missing at the start of this year. It belonged to an elderly couple, holidaying in the Caribbean, the Dunlaps. They went missing along with their boat and still haven't been found."

"Here," Winnie said, handing Frank a printout of the article.

"I don't get it," Frank said. "What has this got to do with Bethany?"

Winnie and Larry exchanged a glance.

"Look, I told her to go to the cops with it," Larry said.

"What did she do?" Frank furrowed his brow.

"I helped her hack in the DHSMV registry."

Frank gave Larry a look.

"I'm not proud of it, okay," Larry said, holding up his hands. "We found the registration for the Dunlap's boat, and said if she could match it to Gilman's boat, she'd know if it were stolen."

Frank felt a sinking feeling in his gut. His eyes narrowed. "What was that name you said?"

"Gilman," Larry said. "Eric Gilman."

Frank's mouth fell open. *How could I be so blind?*

"You okay, detective? You're looking a

267

little…peaked," Winnie said.

"Where is she?" Frank said, grabbing Larry by the arm.

"That's what we've been trying to tell you, detective," Larry said. "We haven't seen Beth since Monday, not since she went to the Marina to check out that boat."

Frank ran a hand through his hair.

Larry snapped his fingers. "Wait, I've got an idea." He returned with his laptop a moment later.

"What's that for?" Frank asked.

Larry smiled. "I can't believe I didn't think of this before. Beth got blackout drunk one weekend and thought she'd lost her phone—turned out it was in the couch cushions at her apartment—but she gave me the password to her cloud account, so we could use the locate missing device feature."

"You think that'll work?" Frank asked.

"Even if her cell phone battery is dead," Larry said, his fingers flying across the keyboard as he hurriedly logged in, "finding the device should be as simple as tracking the last known location."

Frank leaned in.

"Bingo!" Larry said, turning the laptop screen so Frank could see. "She's at the marina."

55

Frank arrived at the marina by late afternoon. He eyed the harbour, a tranquil collection of yachts and floating piers bobbing on an intermittent swell. He stepped over the chained entrance, ignoring the NO TRESPASSING sign, his eyes scanning, looking for potential threats. He was worried about Beth, and angry with himself for not having listened. She'd been right about Dani's boyfriend.

How was I to know he was the unsub? She wanted my help, and I dismissed her.

Frank racked the slide on his Glock, making sure he was cocked and loaded. There was every possibility he might run into El Mohán here. The creature was not to be underestimated: the speed, the phenomenal strength, the capacity for violence. Frank had experienced them firsthand at the shopping mall. El Mohán was responsible for a string of gruesome murders: Chip Kowalski, Helen Werner, the Harris girl. He'd gone through a score of fully trained and armed police officers, at the FLPD, like a hot knife through the proverbial butter. Then, of course, there was Manny and Barnes.

Poor Manny and Barnes.

Further along a wooden walkway, he nearly collided with someone moving in the other direction.

"Stop! Police," Frank said, aiming his gun.

"Woah! Wait," a portly man said. He wore a dishevelled security guard's uniform, and in one of his raised hands, he held a pastry—thankfully, it was only loaded with trans fats.

"Don't shoot," he said.

"Who are you?

"Carl. Marina security."

"Security?" Frank said.

"Sure," Carl said, laughing nervously.

He had a high-pitched laugh which seemed out of place on a man of his stature. "Lots of wealthy people with boats…expensive things on board. Security."

Frank peered behind him at the dockmaster's office. A light shone from inside, and he could see a reception desk with a bank of CCTV displays.

"You got ID?" Carl asked.

Frank obliged him by flashing his badge.

Carl looked relieved. "You almost gave me a heart attack, detective…?"

"Frank Hagen." He relaxed his guard but didn't holster his weapon. "I'm looking for a woman named Bethany Tedesco, Beth for short. She's in her early thirties, about five foot five, with brown hair, and blue eyes. You seen anybody like that?"

Carl cringed. "Only every day—We got maybe one hundred boats here when we're at full capacity. There's a lot of guests who'd match that description."

"She might've been in the company of a man: tall, about six-foot-five, maybe two hundred and twenty pounds."

Carl shrugged.

"Goes by Eric Gilman," Frank added. "He has a boat here, the *Halcyon Daze*?"

"Why didn't you say so?" Carl said. "I can help you with that. If you got a boat that floats, we'll have a record of it. Wait here."

They found the docking space where the *Halcyon Daze* was supposed to be moored. It was vacant. They'd already gone. The swell made empty, lapping sounds against the wooden pilings.

Carl scratched his head.

Frank swore then holstered his gun. *What am I going to do now?*

He caught a glimpse of something, wedged between the gap in the walkway and one of the wooden pilings. It glinted in the sun like a beacon. He reached to grab it, his hand closing around something smooth. *A cell phone!*

Carl raised an eyebrow.

Frank thumbed the screen. A selfie of a young woman throwing a peace sign appeared as the lock screen.

"Beth," Frank said, under his breath.

Carl raised an eyebrow. "She your missing girl?"

Frank nodded. The phone was locked and the battery near dead. "You got a phone charger?"

"Sure, back in the office."

"Can you find out where they were headed?" Frank paced.

"They didn't sign out in the logbook," Carl said.

"We could check the security footage?" pointing to a CCTV camera mounted on a pole.

"They must have left this morning," Carl said, back in the dockmaster's office, while scrubbing through hours of security footage. He pointed to the time stamp.

They'd gone back far enough in the feed to see the stern of the boat magically appear, idling at first, undocking in reverse.

"Stop," Frank said. A man and a woman flashed on the screen, putting out the fenders and making fast the lines.

"Is it them?" Carl asked, wiping the sweat from his brow. It was stuffy in the confined space of the office, despite there being an electric fan.

"That's Gilman alright," Frank said. "Same angular features. Same arrogant posture. I'm not sure about the woman, though. No, wait." (leaning in) He tried to make out the face in the grainy black and white feed. His eyes widened. "That's Dani Kowalski."

"You looking for her, too?" Carl said.

"Not really, but the two women are friends. If she's with Gilman, then there's a good chance that maybe Beth is, too. They're both in danger."

Carl grimaced. "Should we call the coast guard?"

Frank rubbed his face. "Maybe. There's no telling where they've gone." He glanced at Beth's phone, still charging on the counter, and had an idea.

He took out his phone and rang Larry Isles.

56

It's just like before, you're back in the car again. Floating in darkness. Fully immersed. Your lungs are spasming. It's cold. You're sinking fast. You manage to free yourself from your seatbelt. You try the door, but it won't give. You try kicking at the window, but it won't break. Incoherent thoughts go racing inside your head. Is this the end? Feeling faint now. Oh god. So little breath left. You're about to pass out when the door wrenches off its hinges and disappears into the deep. Out of the darkness, a hand reaches in and heaves you out. Someone has you—someone with grayish skin, and webbed-clawed fingers. You're circling the rim of consciousness, but you can tell that much. They have you. It is dark, disorientating, but still they swim upward, following the bubbles to the surface. You hear a hoarse, screaming—Kee-eeeee-arr.

Dani awoke. She'd been lightly dozing aboard the *Halcyon Daze*. There was the smell of the salty ocean brine. They weren't gone long. Maybe three hours. Eric was still at the helm. She'd helped him with the rigging.

It was fun. He'd introduced her to the basics of sailing, tacking, and gybing.

Kee-eeeee-arr.

Dani heard that hoarse cry again. Above, a bird with a large wingspan flew right to the boat, and circled the main mast.

"What is it?" Dani asked.

"A sea hawk," Eric said.

"Why is it doing that?"

He shrugged. "Could be curious, or it could mean there's a storm coming."

The bird flew off and Dani watched it go. There was an eerie calm, and the wind changed. A collection of wispy clouds raced across the sky.

57

"Maybe it'll brush past us?" Eric said, as thunder rumbled. "We might miss the main storm altogether."

They were close-hauled and the sails shuddered. They'd been cruising at eight knots but weren't making any headway. A wall of dark, ominous clouds had formed on the horizon. The air was charged.

"What should we do?" Dani said, teetering as the boat heeled. The wind changed directions, and it started to rain.

"It's too late to run," he said, steering the bow into the waves. "Nothing we can do but ride it out."

Lightning flashed, and the rain turned torrential.

"Should we take down the sail?" Dani asked, the rain whipping her face.

"We'll be fine," he said, rubbing the odd set of creases on his neck. The wind howled in the rigging.

There came a blinding flash followed by a sound like a gunshot. Lightning struck the water next to the boat.

Dani screamed. "That almost hit us!"

Unfazed, Eric kept steering into the waves. "Go below—I got this."

Below deck, it was dark and stuffy. Dani could hear the storm and felt the vibration. She began to cry. This wasn't how she imagined their holiday. She felt for the light switch but—*click, click*—nothing. She tried again. *No luck. Great! What a time for the electricity to give out.*

She felt her way in the dark, steadying herself against the lounge, the polished wooden floor, slippery underfoot. The rain pelted on the butterfly hatch in the ceiling.

Dani pushed off the lounge as the boat rolled again, and grabbed hold of the kitchen counter. She opened the drawers, blindly feeling their contents. *Yess! A flashlight.* The cabin lights came on.

Turning, she spied Eric's laptop on the lounge. Suddenly her curiosity was piqued. *Why did he have all that jewelry? You didn't actually believe his explanation, did you?*

She went to the lounge and powered up the laptop. *Okay, laptop, tell me your secrets.*

First, she looked through the folders and apps, but nothing seemed unusual—it was squeaky clean. Then she came across photos.

Odd. Dani expected to find photos of Eric, or the two of them together, but, instead, she found pictures of strangers: a senior couple, a man and woman in their sixties. The man had weather-beaten skin, like a seasoned mariner, while the woman's hair was dyed a slight shade of blue.

Dani stared at the photos. *Why does Eric have these? Unless…Oh god. What if the laptop isn't his?*

She ran through everything Eric had told her in her mind. *He said he was an art dealer. He'd sailed from Seattle to Lauderdale. Suppose he lied? Oh god. Is this even his boat?*

Breathing heavily, she went to the locker in the main cabin and flung the door open. Among Eric's clothes, she found a couple of hanging zipper bags. Inside the first was a dress, the kind of stylish yet age-appropriate dress that might be worn by a more senior woman. She opened another and found a blue blazer that belonged to a shorter man, much smaller than Eric.

Shit! She closed them. *These aren't his clothes. That isn't his laptop. And this is—not—his—boat. Fuck! I'm in the middle of the ocean with god knows who.* She paced, her hands shaking.

What do I do? I can't let him see me like this.

Forcing herself to take a deep breath, *I've got to go back on deck and pretend like nothing's wrong.*

On her way back through the kitchen, she took a small chopping knife from one of the drawers and concealed it in her sleeve.

58

When Dani came up on deck, the sky was black and the rain was pelting down. The sails had been lowered and the motor was barely audible over the wind.

"Eric," she called, adjusting the knife in her sleeve. He was at the helm dressed in his slicker and hood. "I don't like this. Can we go back?"

Suddenly, a wave hit the starboard side. The boom came loose, swung around and—*CRAACK!*—struck Eric. He let out a startled croak.

"Are you okay?" she said, her voice hoarse from talking over the gale. He hunched over with his back to her.

CRACK-BOOM!—lightning flashed and there was a rumble of thunder. Another wave crashed into the side, dumping water on deck. She inched forward, steadying herself against the railing.

"Eric?" She put a hand on his shoulder.

He flinched and emitted a strange, gurgling noise, his face hidden within the hood of his slicker.

"What's wrong?" she said, startled. "Are you hurt?" reaching with a shaky hand to pull back the hood.

KA-BOOM!—another jolt of thunder followed by a

flash of lightning.

Dani recoiled in horror. The flesh of Eric's face had sloughed away, his features warped into an unspeakably hideous mask—a baleful and grotesque replica. He had transformed into a non-human thing, an abhorrent fish-man, with prodigious bulging eyes and palpitating gills. The folds of its neck opened and closed, gasping in unison. Its mouth stretched wide, displaying rows of sharp teeth.

Dani froze, her heart hammering in her chest. *No! No, no.* She was sure she would go insane from fright. There was a—*Rrrip!*—and a row of savage-looking spines sprouted from its back.

Dani gave an ear-shattering scream. She realized this was the thing that haunted her dreams since childhood. She remembered…*Floating inside the capsizing car. The door wrenched from its hinges. Something with grayish skin, swimming her towards the surface.*

Her mind snapped back to the present.

"D-don't be scared," it said in a guttural, croaking voice. "I am not this…this thing. I am here. I have waited nearly all your life—" It reached for her with a webbed-clawed hand.

Remembering the knife hidden in her sleeve, Dani slashed at the thing, but its tough skin deflected the blow. It let out croaking bark, and, quick as a flash, pitched the knife over the side.

"No, Dani. I love you," it said.

Dan screamed, trying to push it away, but its mucus-covered skin was too slippery. She kicked at it and dashed towards the stern.

There came an unearthly, high-pitched—*Whoop!*—

and it tried to grapple her.

She screamed again and half leaped, half slid down the companionway, below deck. There was a burst of pain as her ankle rolled, and she landed in a heap at the foot of the stairs.

The moments seemed to lag as she lay on the cabin floor, the pain in her ankle was excruciating. *I must've sprained it.* She willed herself to stand.

The hatch!

Quick as she could, she limped to the top of the stairs and shut the door. The creature lunged—*SLAM!* The door strained as the creature tried to force its way in.

"Leave me alone!" Dani said, precariously balanced, doing her best to bolster the door with her shoulder while gripping the handrail.

"Da-ani!" it cried.

SLAM! SLAM.

She felt the ungodly strength of the thing with each attempt. *Oh god. Jesus. That thing is Eric.* The door nearly buckled, then the banging stopped.

She backed away, feeling as if she'd stumbled into a waking nightmare. Looking about frantically, she saw it...

The radio!

She limped to the navigation station, where the VHF radio was built into the panelling. There was a red distress button. She pressed it, hoping it might connect her to the coastguard, but nothing happened.

No, no, no.

She snatched the speaker. "Hello, hello...This is Dani Kowalski on board the *Halcyon Daze*. Help. Please. Can anyone hear me? Mayday!" When she released the talk button, there was only silence.

"Shit!" She threw the speaker down. *The lightning must have blown out the radio.*

SLAM, SLAM—the creature began its assault on the companionway doors again. They rattled and shook, and Dani prayed the latch would hold.

Regaining composure, she limped to the kitchen and snatched another knife from one of the drawers. *Too small. There has to be—*

SLAM, SLAM——the creature charged again.

Dani checked the other drawers, but there was nothing useful. Out of frustration, she turned over the lounge cushions and found, hidden underneath, between the lifejackets, a small plastic briefcase.

She felt a surge of hope as she opened the clasps. Inside, resting in gray-plastic-foam, she found a pistol-shaped flare launcher with four red, plastic shells.

SLAM, SLAM—went the doors again, accompanied by the sound of splintering wood.

That door won't hold?

She took the flare launcher and hurriedly loaded one of the shells, pocketing the others. *How am I going to get out of here?* glancing about the room. *The butterfly hatch*!

Tucking the flare gun into her pant line, she climbed onto the kitchen table. She reached, but the hatch was too high for her, even on tiptoe. Using the plastic briefcase to stand on, she tried again. It slid with each motion of the boat. *It's no good.* Her fingers barely touched the edges of the hatch.

In desperation, she stood the briefcase vertically on its end. She tried again. It wobbled, and she steadied herself with her hands on the ceiling. The hatch opened.

I did it! feeling the cold from outside on her face.

Dani heaved herself through the hatch just as the companionway doors were breached, her head and shoulders outside, while her legs dangled below.

Suddenly, she felt the vice-like grip of the creature's hands on her leg, its claws digging through the denim of her jeans. She shrieked and kicked blindly, until it let go.

The creature gazed up at her and bellowed, as she lay amidships, on her belly, panting.

C'mon. Get up. Dani rose and looked about desperately. She hoped she might see land, but saw nothing but vast ocean. The partially reefed mainsail fluttered above them in the maelstrom.

A moment later, the creature appeared on deck, looking monstrous. There was an intelligence behind its eyes, and she knew it was Eric. It stretched to its full height and gave a high-pitched—*Whoop!*

"Stay away!" Dani drew the flare launcher and aimed.

It lunged, colliding with her as she pulled the trigger, knocking the launcher from her hand, but not before a phosphorescent, red flare hissed into the mainsail. Everything was suddenly bathed in an eerie, red incandescence.

Dani teetered against the railing but couldn't stop herself. She was weightless, falling, and clutched at the air but to no avail. She ricocheted off something solid on the way down and plunged into the darkness of the water below.

59

Dani's heart raced as she fought against the current. *Jesus. Please don't let me die like this.* She caught glimpses of the boat's lights with each undulation of the waves. It drew further away with each passing second.

She tried a crawling, swimming stroke, alternating each arm, but had trouble coordinating her muscles. Her fingertips touched something—*a rope!*—it must have been trailing from the back of the boat, and she instinctively grabbed hold. It went taut, and she was towed.

Turning her head to breathe, she saw the boat's dinghy, overturned, all its contents floating by. A wave dunked her and she slid back several feet, the rope nearly slipping from her grasp. *Oh, fuckfuckfuck.* If she let go, it would spell the end for her. Without a life preserver, what chance did she have?

Slipping back several more feet, she discovered the rope was tied to a bulky, canvas-wrapped object. Dani clung to it, as a fold of the material shifted, revealing a matt of curly, brown hair and...a face.

"Oh, God, no. Beth!" Dani wailed, clinging to the body of her dead friend. She couldn't understand what she was seeing. Reaching to touch Beth's sunken cheek, her head lolled.

"Wake up!" Dani said, before a wave pushed them under. She resurfaced a moment later, coughing and spluttering.

Beth had tried to warn her about Eric. Was it possible she'd discovered the truth about him? Had he killed her for it?

I should have listened to you, Beth. I'm sorry.

The rope and canvas unravelled and they went into a spin. Luckily, Dani caught hold of the rope once more. But, as the canvas unfurled, Beth's body was set adrift.

"No!" Dani cried, watching helplessly as Beth bobbed away with the current, fading into the black. She couldn't believe her friend was gone. *Eric did this.* Her body tensed. She needed to get back aboard. She needed to survive.

It was as if a switch flipped in Dani's brain. Adrenaline took over. She hauled herself along the rope, her limbs extending, her muscles straining. It was slow-going, the wet cord rubbing the inside of her palms raw. Seawater filled her mouth and stung her eyes. Steadily she made progress, and found herself towed directly behind the stern.

She eyed the railing—it looked so far out of reach. With her remaining strength, she hoisted herself up and over the top, collapsing onto the deck, coughing and spluttering.

She lay there with her eyes closed, panting, trying to collect her thoughts. It was a miracle she'd made it. Where was the creature? She'd half-expected it to pounce. *Maybe it thinks I drowned?*

Dani became aware of a flickering light, and her

eyes snapped open. To her dismay, she realized the *Halcyon Daze* was on fire.

The flare! It had caught fire to the sail.

She watched as flames leaped and burned. Black smoke billowed.

Dani stood, slowly. The boat's motor could still be heard over the storm. *What am I going to do?* She scanned the deck.

The creature appeared and let out another— *WHOOP!*

"Fuck you!" Dani screamed, clenching her fists.

It leaped and took a swipe at Dani with its webbed-claws.

Dani dodged and fell to the floor of the cockpit. Something caught her eye: *the flare launcher!* It had skittered across the deck, and nestled behind the helm. She pat her pocket and was amazed to find one of the shells was still there.

She grabbed the launcher, then rolled—narrowly avoiding another of the creature's attacks. Dani lay on her back and reloaded the launcher with shaky hands. She inserted one of the flares.

It has to work. Please.

She pointed the launcher and fired. *Yesss!* The flare hit the creature full force in the chest, and it let out a startled, inhuman cry.

It stumbled back against the railing, an expression of disbelief in its fish-like eyes. It pawed at the burning flare in its chest, teetered, then fell.

SPLASH!

Dani felt a wave of relief. *Oh, thank God. Did I kill it? I think I killed it. It's over.* Exhausted, she dropped the flare launcher and looked at the clouds. She felt betrayed, violated. *That thing was Eric*. The thought sickened her. The rain pelted down while the masthead burned, the flames licking and devouring, at once beautiful and terrifying.

60

Frank telephoned Larry Isles, Beth's work colleague, and asked him to come to the marina with his laptop. He'd been helpful earlier, when Frank called in at the office. It was plain to see he cared for Beth—they were friends. The man had volunteered, and Frank needed his assistance. Not only was Larry a massive geek, but he had a boating license. He pulled up in his step-dad's cabin cruiser about an hour or so later, wearing Bermuda shorts, Hawaiian shirt fluttering in the breeze.

"Yippee-ki-yay, motherfucker," he said.

Frank chuckled.

On board the boat, Larry fired up his laptop.

"I need you to hack into this," Frank said, handing him Beth's cell phone. "Beth and Dani were BFFs, so maybe there's something there which can tell us where they went."

"No problem," Larry said, after looking it over briefly. "I'll first log into her cloud account to see if she's synchronized her messages."

"Nope," he said a moment later.

Frank sighed. "Any other ideas?"

Larry stroked his chin. "Let me check—aha! This

particular model has a vulnerability. If I go to the lock screen, open the phone's 'Emergency Call' feature, type in a few characters, then copy-and-paste repeatedly, I'll overload and crash the system, which will take us back to the unlocked screen." He laughed.

"I'm impressed," Frank said.

"It's what I do," Larry said, polishing his fingernails on his lapel.

He was *in* within minutes and handed the phone to Frank.

Frank scrolled. "Beth's last message to Dani was on Monday. 'We need to talk,'" he said, reading the message aloud. He looked up. "That's nearly three days ago; around the time I got that voicemail from her."

Larry rubbed the back of his neck.

"Dani checked in a couple of times after that," Frank said, scrolling further, "but no response from Beth."

Larry's face tightened. "That's not great, is it?"

Frank frowned, stopped scrolling, and smiled. "At least we know where they're headed."

Larry raised an eyebrow.

"Dani sent a text message. Gilman's taking her to Key West. Can we make it there in this boat? They've got a sizeable lead on us."

"It's a stretch," Larry said. "Could be pretty hairy if we run into any bad conditions. Still, we have extra fuel cans on board, water, food. Maybe we'll get lucky, and catch them up."

The cabin cruiser made its way through the chop, out to sea. Larry was at the wheel. Frank leaned against the rail, staring at the horizon, as if the act itself would manifest the *Halcyon Daze.*

Frank braced, as they cut across the swell. He'd been on his feet for nearly twelve hours. He rubbed the spot of his old leg wound. His stomach grumbled, and he had a dry mouth. He was worried about Beth. He hadn't seen her in the CCTV video back at the dock, but that didn't mean she wasn't aboard the *Halcyon Daze.* He was worried for Danny, too. El Mohán was a butcher. It was only a matter of time before she'd wind up another of his victims. *God, I hope we're not too late.*

"Do you think we'll find them?" Frank said.

"Huh?" Larry said, steering across the waves.

The wind buffeted and the motor roared.

"Will—we—find—them?"

"No," Larry said, shaking his head, frowning.

"We have to try!"

Larry nodded, throttled back, and increased speed. He handed Frank a pair of binoculars.

Frank took them, peering out in the dark, hopeful he might see the lights of the other boat. He swore. *Like trying to find a needle in a haystack.*

Frank looked up. Above them was a single gray cloud, which quickly expanded and coalesced, until it covered everything, obscuring all the stars in the night sky. The air felt heavy, moist, and the wind changed direction.

"We could be in for it," Larry said, nodding towards an anvil-shaped bank of clouds, which continued to boil and climb upwards.

Frank joined Larry by the wheel.

As if on cue, there was a flash of lightning and a massive boom of thunder. The sky opened and it rained down in sheets.

Several hours later, and they were in the middle of one of the biggest storms Frank had ever experienced. Their little cabin cruiser was dwarfed by ginormous waves. The wind roared and howled.

"We have to turn back!" Larry said, doing his best to steer through the monstrous waves. His face was ashen.

"What's that?" Frank pointed.

Larry squinted. "It looks like a vessel?"

As they got closer, they realized it was the *Halcyon Daze*. It was ablaze, flames visible in the darkness, smoke and embers drifting upwards. Each roll of the swell threatened to capsize her.

Larry manoeuvred them alongside and tried to hail them on the radio. Nothing. Nothing stirred. He gave a long blast of the boat horn.

"Hello!" Frank called. "Is anybody aboard?"

61

On a cool November evening, Dani stood in the kitchen of her Dorland Park home, steam issuing from a pot on the stove, a Bowie track playing in the background. Adding oregano and garlic to a mixture she stirred in a pan, she leaned in and inhaled the delicious aroma. A timer went off. She set the sauce aside and placed the pasta into a colander.

The nightmare was over. It had been months since her entanglement with Eric—*or was it El Mohán?* Frank had rescued her from the *Halcyon Daze*. She was still having nightmares, but they weren't like the recurrent nightmares of her youth. Perhaps, this was a byproduct of El Mohán's death. He wasn't there to exert his influence.

She'd found a new therapist—it had been necessary. Buchinsky wasn't able to take her back as a client. He'd experienced a psychotic break and needed therapy himself. She was dealing with the losses in her life: Chip, Beth, her parents. She'd experienced more than her fair share. That much was certain.

Grief was a funny thing: she would be going along okay for a while, but then, would see a photo, or hear a song lyric, and would break down crying. It was a process, and she was still going through it.

She missed Chip—despite all the bullshit and instability he'd caused in her life. She'd loved him, in her way.

Pouring herself a glass of wine, she moved to the studio, where her latest work stood on an easel. It was a self-portrait, bright and colorful—unlike anything she'd painted before. The Dani in the painting wore a contented smile, projecting an air of confidence. It was a hopeful piece, full of promise.

Dani was earning a decent income as an artist. Not enough to go full-time, but enough to supplement her main income. She sold art prints through an online store—Larry had helped her set it up; had some commission work; and an exhibition due in the fall. She would need to downsize to a condo, and would have to keep working at the diner, but that was okay.

She took a sip of wine and thought of Beth. She missed her every day. She'd been like a sister, a confidant. No longer would she hear her friend's laughter or jokes. It wasn't fair.

The events of the past few months had been horrific. Dani realized Eric—*El Mohán*—had been responsible for a string of murders from the time they first met. It was unbelievable. The more time elapsed, the less it seemed real. It was as if it happened to someone else. If it weren't for Frank and Larry, she might have doubted her sanity.

El Mohán might have rescued her as a child, but as an adult, it seemed like he'd meant to torment her.

The phone rang and she moved back to the kitchen to answer it. It was Frank. It was good to hear his voice.

"Hey, where are you?" she asked.

"I'm on my way."

Dani could hear the sounds of the checkout and the supermarket in the background.

She stopped.

The screen door to the back yard was open. *Strange.* She couldn't remember leaving it open.

"I made a detour to get the ice cream you like," Frank said. "They didn't have any at the Stop & Shop."

Dani was amused. Not for the first time, she realized she was falling for him. What had started as friendship—just two lonely people enjoying each other's company—was becoming something more. There was an attraction there. They'd been through a lot together, but were taking things slow.

Dani flipped the latch and locked the screen door. The waters of the bay twinkled in the moonlight. She wasn't afraid of the water anymore.

"You there still?" he asked.

"Huh?—I'm sorry. I blanked," she said, getting emotional. "I was thinking about…you know?"

"Hey, we promised, we weren't going to dwell on the past, remember?"

"You're right," she said, wiping the tears from her cheek.

"So, what movie did you pick for us to watch?" he asked, changing the subject.

She sniffed. "*Notting Hill.*"

"Never seen it. Is it good?"

"You serious? Hugh Grant. Julia Roberts. You'll love it. Just hurry up and get here."

***

By the time Frank arrived, the stars were out and the street outside Dani's home was bathed in moonlight. The house was dark except for the lighted windows. A tall palm tree stood, looming, casting a long shadow. Cutting the engine, he grabbed the shopping bag, removed his off-duty weapon from the glove box, and stepped from the car.

Walking up the drive, he thought about the strange events that had led him there. It had been months since his run-in with El Mohán—since his world had turned on its head.

Frank and Dani had found each other in the aftermath. She was special to him and was a comfort during a dark time. He was glad to have her in his life.

He stepped to the porch and knocked on the door. Nothing stirred inside the house. "Hello—Dani?"

Still no movement.

Frank tried her cell, but she didn't answer. He peered in the window, but the curtains were drawn. *Where is she?* Instinct told him something was wrong. They had been talking on the phone, not ten minutes ago. He felt a sinking feeling in his stomach, and his mouth was dry.

Setting down the shopping bag, he took out his gun—a Glock like his on-duty weapon. Frank knocked again. *Why doesn't she answer? Dammit.*

He kicked in the door.

"Dani?!" he said, scanning the hallway for threats. "If you're there—say something." He hoped it was a false alarm.

The house was quiet—too quiet. It felt abandoned. Frank's heart beat faster. Padding across the carpet to the kitchen, he found a shattered wine glass. *Something's wrong.* He placed a hand over the pot on the stove. *Still warm.*

Returning to the hall, he moved from room to room, clearing them, sweeping his gun from side to side.

Passing Dani's studio, he was startled by the outline of a shape in the corner of the room. It turned out to be just one of Dani's paintings on an easel.

Ascending the stairs, his old leg wound ached, and the most intense feeling of déjà vu came over him. It was as if he were in a waking dream.

From inside one of the bedrooms, he heard a muffled sound. He took a breath, tightened his grip on his gun, and opened the door.

The room was dark and the window was open. Danni was standing there but was not alone. There was a dark shape. *Movement. What is that?* It was El Mohán.

"Don't you fucking hurt her!" Frank said.

The creature stood behind Dani with a webbed hand over her mouth, a powerful arm around her waist. She whimpered. Frank could see the terror in her eyes.

"Let her go!" Frank said.

The thing chuckled, amused, its large fish-like eyes, black and lifeless.

"Maybe it's *me* you want, huh?" Frank said. "Do you want a piece of me? What if I put the gun down and we duke this out, mano a mano?"

El Mohán laughed. "You'd—like—that," it said in an inhuman, gravely voice.

Frank stared at Dani, willing her to move.

Taking the cue, she bit down hard on the creature's hand and slipped to the side.

Frank raised his gun and fired—*BANG!*—Nothing

happened.

The creature roared and rushed him.

Frank shot a second time—again, nothing happened. He swung at the creature, but it deftly avoided the blow. It struck him and hurled him backwards into the closet mirror, showering Frank in broken glass fragments.

62

El Mohán bellowed, dealing a blow to Dani's head. She teetered for a moment before blacking out. The creature scooped her onto its shoulders in a fireman's carry, and leaped through the open window into the night.

"No. Noooo!" Frank yelled, trying to blink away stars, wiping a trickle of blood from his chin. He snatched his gun and scrambled for the window. It had to be a twenty-foot drop. El Mohán had landed, adroitly, on a patch of grass and ran in the direction of the neighbor's yard, with Dani still on its shoulders.

Frank holstered his weapon and clambered out the window, across uneven tiles. Reaching the gutter, he let his legs hang until he found a toehold and slid down the nearest downpipe.

Once on the ground, he stooped to catch his breath. He was already sore and fatigued. *Where are they?* The moonlight shone, and he could make out a trail of blue blood across the yard. *It's hurt.* Frank allowed himself to hope, straightened, and gave chase.

Settling into a loping run, his feet pounded the ground while his heart hammered. *How can it move so fast?* Up ahead, there was a shadow-like blur.

"Stop!" he yelled, as they disappeared into a hedge. He lowered his head and barged through to a clearing on the other side. He glimpsed them as it finished scaling a wire-mesh fence, dropping into a void, below.

Frank swore after colliding with the fence. He struck it with his fist. Beyond was an open trench drain, a grotto-like, cement canal. El Mohán was in the middle-distance, splashing through ankle-deep, graywater in the direction of the bay—in the direction of the Atlantic.

I can't let it get away.

Frank climbed, pushing with his feet while extending his arms. He vaulted the top, but hesitated before dropping and landed awkwardly. The fall sent shockwaves through his bad leg, and he collapsed into the brackish water, grunting in pain.

The water stank of decomposition and household waste. Something in his leg had given out. *C'mon. Get up!* he thought, forcing himself to stand. The pain was excruciating.

El Mohán was ahead, retreating with Dani on its shoulder. Frank heard its echoing footfalls. The murky water glimmered in the moonlight.

Frank ran, but each step felt like jabbing needles, burning pain radiating outwards.

"STOP!" Frank yelled, drawing his gun and firing in the air.

El Mohán ignored him.

"If you ever loved her," Frank said, "you'd let her go!"

It stopped, turned, and jeered. The thing tilted its head and let out a long, whooping bark.

Frank aimed. He wanted to shoot, but there was a

chance he'd hit Dani.

"Let—her—go," Frank said.

The thing looked at him with black, dish-like eyes that glinted, full of hate. It made a rasping, cackling sound, resembling laughter, backtracked, and placed Dani on a ledge. She was unconscious but otherwise unharmed.

Why come back? Frank realized it had unfinished business. It hated him and wanted him dead. He'd impugned its precious pride.

El Mohán squared up to fight, stretching to its full, intimidating height. It let out a bloodcurdling— *WHOOP, WHOOP!*—followed by a hooting bark.

Frank noticed blue blood oozing from its side. *If it bleeds, I can hurt it.*

It pounced with lightning speed, knocking the gun from Frank's hand and slashing his chest. Frank flinched, but landed an elbow to the creature's body. It stumbled backwards with a look of surprise on its face.

A retractable, bone-like spike extended from El Mohán's hand. It sprang forward, stabbing, but Frank jammed the attack with his forearms.

It tried to pull Frank onto the venom-filled spike, but Frank resisted. Grunting with exertion, he could feel his bad leg about to give. It was a contest of wills. He dropped and struck the creature where it had been wounded.

The thing roared and kicked at Frank, sending him splashing into the graywater. In no time, the thing was on top, holding Frank down while he thrashed and kicked underwater, desperate for air.

Frank opened his eyes underwater and saw his gun. *Need to...reach.* His fingertips touched the gun handle, but he couldn't grab it.

Suddenly El Mohán's hand released, and Frank could reach the gun. "Argh!" Frank spluttered, breaking to the surface, gasping for air.

He saw Dani. She had regained consciousness and had stabbed El Mohán in the neck with a shard of mirror.

"I hate you!" she screamed, stabbing over and over.

An expression of puzzlement flashed across El Mohán's face, blue blood spurting from its neck in a geyser. It realized for the first time it was mortal.

It started to transform, changing back into a man. It was Eric Gilman again. "Dani?" it spluttered. "I love you…I always have?"

Dani looked at him and said, "I—DON'T—CARE!"

Frank fired—*BANG, BANG, BANG!*

El Mohán staggered, looking first at Dani, then Frank, then back at Dani again. Its visage flickered like a malfunctioning hologram, its gills working, opening and closing, desperate for breath. It fell back, shriveled, dying, until it dissipated, becoming one with the brackish water.

EPILOGUE

Weeks later…

Dani stood in the bathroom, fixing her hair.

"Are you ready?" Frank asked.

"Almost," she said. "What time's the reservation?"

"One o'clock."

They had moved in together. It made sense. They were saving money on the rent, and it meant that Frank wouldn't be going back and forth from his apartment.

Dani stopped. She suddenly felt nauseous.

She took a couple of deep breaths.

"Are you okay?"

"Yeah, fine," Dani said. She gagged then made a rush for the toilet.

She vomited, coughing and spluttering.

Frank went and rubbed her back in a comforting gesture. "Jeez, you poor thing. You might have the flu."

"No, seriously. I'm fine—" Dani vomited again.

"Look, I'll call the guys and cancel, okay?"

"Okay, sure. You're right," Dani said.

She watched him leave the room.

As he spoke on the phone in the hall, Dani tried to

remember when she last had her period. She was late.

No, please don't be pregnant.

She stood side-on to the mirror, and rubbed her belly. Was it her imagination or had her breasts grown bigger?

What if I'm pregnant? Would that be so terrible? Frank and I are in a good place. We love each other. But then thought, *What if the baby's El Mohán's?*

ABOUT THE AUTHOR

Brent McGregor is the writer of over three books, including *Blood Tide*, *Strange Murmurings*, and *Denizens of Darkhaven*. He is a prizewinning author of horror and dark fiction, a member of the AHWA, and lives in Sydney with his wife, daughter, and dogs. His work has appeared in the Australasian Horror Writers' Association publication, *Midnight Echo*. And he is the winner of the 2024 Asylumfest Mayday Hills Ghost Story Competition. Brent likes to delve into the world of the terrifying by writing stories that combine both the weird and the uncanny.

Visit him online at BrentMcGregor.com and join his newsletter, or follow him on Instagram or Facebook.

ACKNOWLEDGEMENTS

Writing a novel is harder than I thought, but more rewarding than I could have imagined. None of this would have been possible without my wife, Amy. She is patient and understanding, a wonderful mother, and quite honestly the best person I know. Thank you, darling, for your incredible heart and invaluable support.

I would like to thank my daughter, Roxanne, for her boundless energy and infectious spirit. You bring so much joy to our lives.

I would also like to thank my parents, Stephen and Glynne, for their love, support, and guidance.

A very special thank you to my writing group and critique partners, the NightQuills (Jeff Clulow, Alister Hodge, Georgina Ballantine, and David-Jack Fletcher), who have been instrumental in helping me to reach this point.